About the author

PEADAR O'DONNELL was born in 1893 on the sea-coast of County Donegal in northwestern Ireland. Throughout a long life he has been well known in his own country both as a novelist and as a revolutionary. He was in IRA headquarters in the Dublin Four Courts when Ireland's first civil war started in 1922. He has written three volumes of autobiography and seven novels, each of them, in his own words, 'brewed from experience.'

THE PLOT

ULSTER in 1912. In the border territory of Donegal Protestant farmers of the rich Lagan valley confront the hill-farmers of Catholic Gaeldom, driven out from the lands their ancestors once owned. There is consternation as a Catholic family, the Godfrey Dhus, buys into the Protestant enclave.

In far-off Dublin the Easter Rising takes place, and the 'Troubled Times' spread through the Irish countryside. Insurrection is followed by civil war.

'Knife' Godfrey Dhu is at the centre of the fight on the Republican side and fiery red-headed Nuala Godfrey Dhu is its inspiration. She is courted by Catholic Phil Byrne, Protestant Sam Rowan and the wistful, fair-minded Doctor Henry. Which of them will carry the day?

Peadar O'Donnell from the drawing by Sean O'Sullivan

From the same publishers:

A PROSE AND VERSE ANTHOLOGY OF MODERN IRISH WRITING
Edited by Grattan Freyer, with Preface by Conor Cruise O'Brien. 320 pp.

Also available:

PEADAR O'DONNELL
By Grattan Freyer. 128 pp. (Bucknell University Press)

THE KNIFE

BY

PEADAR O'DONNELL

Author of *Islanders* and *Adrigoole*

IRISH HUMANITIES CENTRE

23 Westland Row, Dublin 2, and
Keohanes Ltd., Ballina and Sligo
1980

First published in Great Britain in 1930 by
Jonathan Cape Ltd. and in America by
Jonathan Cape & Harrison Smith Inc.

This edition © published in 1980 by Irish
Humanities Centre, Ltd., 23 Westland Row, Dublin 2,
and Keohanes Ltd., Ballina and Sligo, Ireland

ISBN 0-906462-02-9 cloth
ISBN 0-906462-03-7 paper

Reproduced from copy supplied
printed and bound in Great Britain
by Billing and Sons Limited
Guildford, London, Oxford, Worcester

THE KNIFE

TO

THE SEÁN MÓRS

CHAPTER ONE

Sam Rowan's farm was in the centre of a compact planter district. Every rood of land was owned by a solid Orange stock. It was said of the Rowans that a native never slept under their roof nor broke bread at their table. Their servant men were housed and fed in a loft over the stable.

William Rowan was old, wasted, asthmatic. He sat in his chair in the corner, leaning forward so that he could spit easily into the fire. He was alone. Rebecca had gone down to Richard Gregg to see whether he could ease her mind of this rumour. William leaned forward and coughed and waited. He took up the tongs and drew aimless strokes in the ashes, his bushy eyebrows poked forward, his cheeks puffing out and in as he breathed. His skin was puckered, kippered, tawny. His eyes were sunken and wide and bright, his hair bristling, short cropped, speckled.

He waited in patience. Rebecca would be back soon. He rested the tongs against the wall and turned to keep his eye on the open door. A hen thrust her head in and turned one questioning eye on William, took a step forward, halted with one foot in the air, her head twisted round to catch a sound outside, and then with a jerk of her wings swung round and disappeared.

A big, black, long-haired dog, with dull eye and heavy step, came softly in. He looked around listlessly, wagged his tail lazily, and ambled over to a dish of hens' meat, nosed it, pulled his lips apart, and nibbled listlessly at a piece of the feed, dropped it, and walked lazily out. In the doorway he halted, one ear slightly raised, his tail again wagging slowly. William sat up straight and leaned towards the door, his hand cupped behind his ear to catch the message in any sound outside. Sitting for years in a corner had made William keen on sounds. When Rebecca's hard-heeled tramp caught his ear he breathed in sharply.

Rebecca came quickly in; she came up and sat down on the chair opposite him, and jerked her head backward on her lean, wrinkled neck.

'It's true,' she said, breathlessly, her stiffened arms reaching down between her knees, her fingers locked, her breathing laboured.

William looked quickly away; he stared into the fire. His fingers sought the tongs; he prodded the turf; he let the tongs fall; he uncrossed his legs, swung a limp leg back over a withered knee; jerked his slippered foot up and down; cleared his throat; glanced back at Rebecca; and then suddenly slouching forward in his chair, he picked up the tongs and drew strokes in the ashes.

'Am no' understandin' it,' he said quietly, almost to himself.

'It's devil's work,' Rebecca said angrily.

William looked up sharply. Anger surprised him, for William had only been troubled.

'Who would ye be blamin'?' he asked her.

'I dunno,' she said, getting to her feet. 'I dunno, but there's somebody.' She sat down again.

'We'll just ha' to wait till Sammy comes.' His cough returned. Rebecca sat motionless, her body stiff, her eyes staring unseeingly at the wall.

The dog made faint throatal greetings, and William's cough snapped quickly. Rebecca and he sat straight up and stared at the door. Sam Rowan came in. He was a big-framed man, now in the middle twenties. His eyes went straight to his aunt and father at the fireside: brown eyes with a cold tone in them. He hung his cap on a peg on the wall, took off his coat, and sat down to unloose his shoes.

'It's true then, Sammy,' Rebecca said, rising, her hands crushed against her breast.

Sam nodded. With his boots loose he moved towards the room door, struggling to undo his collar stud as he walked.

Rebecca sat down again; her hands were now limp in her lap. The stiffness left old William's body too; he leaned forward in his chair and coughed.

Men returning from the fair yelled in the roadway. Sam came down from the room in his socked feet, and he was now in his working clothes. He sought under the kitchen table for his heavy boots. Rebecca got wearily to her feet to set his dinner on the table.

Sam ate in silence. Rebecca went out into the yard. The old man drew strokes in the ashes with the tongs.

CHAPTER TWO

THE news had burst on the fair without any warning for when the Godfrey Dhus had begun to work around Montgomerys, clearing up the walk, mending the roof, fixing gates and doing work inside, nobody was very much interested. The Godfrey Dhus were servant men who often took contracts. Last year they had put the Major's lodge in order, for The Knife was as good as any carpenter, folk said, although he had never been taught anything beyond what he picked up attending tradesmen here and there. Old Godfrey Dhu himself was a good worker in stone, and his two boys, The Knife and Hugh, took after him in that, so that it was natural they should have taken on the job of tightening things up around Montgomerys. It was years since the absentee owner had put in an appearance, and whether he intended to appear again or not, it was to his interest to keep the place from going to ruin.

Billy White had seen them there, of course, and he champed his jaws and passed on to look after his cattle, growling softly to himself. Sam Rowan had seen them there, and stopped to ask The Knife to come and try the pace of a new horse he had bought. He had waved his hand to Nuala, who had appeared in the doorway to call the men to a meal; sensible idea to have her come over and cook for the men on the job, he thought, as he drove away; good for the house, too, to have a fire in it. A bright sapling of a woman, he found himself thinking, as he turned to close the gate, and he looked up again sharply, but she was gone.

Godfrey Dhu himself was stamping up the walk; powerful trunk of a man, Godfrey Dhu. Sam recalled suddenly that he had heard that Godfrey Dhu had drawn a plough, and he could well believe it. He paused with the reins in his hand to look back, with the ploughing incident in his mind, but Godfrey had gone, and he thought again of Nuala. He stepped into the cart and drove off.

Sam Rowan had come close to Nuala Godfrey Dhu one other evening when she strolled among the trees around Montgomerys. She was singing as he drew near, and he walked softly for fear she might end the song. He stood in the shelter of an old tree while she came slowly towards him. Sam had heard little singing beyond hymns on a Sunday, and certainly he had never heard a voice like this. He peeped under the branches; she was standing on the path looking out, through a clearing in the trees, on to the fields of the Lagan. And his mind gave heed to the words, and as he listened the music ceased to give him pleasure. It was a Fenian song she was singing. 'The dark-minded wee bitch,' he muttered, and stamped along on his way. He did not notice that the song broke off suddenly, for his mind was still resenting the words of that song; they were all alike, these servant men and women; just filled up to the neck with badness; can't sing anything but Fenian songs, he fumed. He cut out on the road, and strode past Doctor Henry, who was fishing a hole in the river.

'Whither goeth Goliath?' the Doctor challenged. 'You looked like you were going out to battle as you came along.'

'Well, maybe,' Sam agreed, coming towards the Doctor.

'And what was bothering you?'

'Oh, just a bit of a song.'

'Nuala beyond? Fine voice that girl.'

'Aye, 'twas Nuala.'

The Doctor made a cast; a trout flicked the water with his tail.

'He's a beauty, that boy, but saucy; we've been waving to each other for an hour.' Further up along the river somebody began to whistle. The Doctor paused in his cast, and smiled. 'Young Tommy Smith that's whistling,' he said.

'Aye, young Tommy,' Sam said.

'What's this you call that tune?' the Doctor asked.

'Your wee-while in England must ha' cut chunks out of ye if ye no min' *Derry Walls*.

'Aye, just so, *Derry Walls*,' he said with a grin.

'Well, it's a likely enough thing to whistle,' Sam said.

'Aye, Sammy. Jumping snakes! A beauty! I have him; jump, ye devil. Oh, Dolly's brae, oh, Dolly's brae. . . . Listen to him, Sam; music; cold water and a string of gut! Atta boy; jump; easy boy, easy; only holding by a hair; easy boy, easy; brain that dog, Sam; oh, you beauty!'

'Shut up, Doctor Henry,' Nuala called, arriving at

a run. 'Land your fish; I never knew a man to talk – Oh, my poor fellow! Make a dash, jump, jump!'

'Shut up, you hussy, or I'll brain you.'

'Jump! Make a hoop and snap!'

'Sam, pitch her in the river,' Doctor Henry urged.

'Hurrah! Oh, my poor, big fellow!'

After one last plunge the fish stood steady. The Doctor reeled in slowly, the fish was deep down. Nuala on a flag was gazing down into the river. Sam Rowan was tapping his legging with the gaff. The Doctor continued to reel in carefully. Suddenly the fish shot straight for the surface and rose high into the air. The Doctor, in tilting backwards, stumbled against Sam; the rod jerked violently, and the fish spun round in the air, and flopped back into the water, free. Nuala clapped her hands and cheered. The Doctor sat down on the bank.

'Don't cry, Doctor Henry, I'll give you a glass marble and a bit of string.'

'I could break your back, Nuala.'

'Let it be a warning to you not to sing party tunes when you're fishing Irish salmon; they don't like it.'

'Who was singing party tunes?'

'Well, not singing, but you were roaring *Dolly's Brae*.'

'I wasn't, Nuala!'

''Deed were you.'

'Well, I'm damned.'

Nuala glanced at Sam where he stood silently by the river. 'I'm glad he escaped,' she said. 'Still, he was a beauty.'

'Run, or I'll fling something at you,' the Doctor threatened.

Nuala laughed, made a face at him, and passed on.

'Going over to the shop,' the Doctor said, explaining her presence to himself.

'She's a forward bit of a strumpet,' Sam Rowan said.

'Don't be an ass, Sam Rowan. Did you ever see such a damn fine head of rusty hair,' he added.

'There's venom under it; you should hear the meanin' she was puttin' into that song.'

'Oh, my righteous Covenanter! Listen to the row young Tommy Smith is making with the *Boyne Water*. An' she says I was roaring *Dolly's Brae*; me!'

'Aye, and why not you?'

'I will even cast my fly again,' the Doctor said, getting to his feet. 'And run along, Sam, like a good boy, and take off your boots and catch minnows with your toes. By the way, Sam,' the Doctor called after his cousin, before he had disappeared round the bend, 'aren't the Godfrey Dhus a long time about Montgomerys?'

'The Godfrey Dhus are all right,' Sam said back over his shoulder; he was feeling grumpy with the Doctor. 'I suppose they're all the same,' he grumbled as he walked off.

'Sam!'

'Well?'

'Hasn't she a damn fine voice?'

'Never heard anything like it,' Sam enthused. 'The voice is all right,' he grumbled, after a pause. The Doctor flicked his cast across the river, and Sam strode off through the fields.

CHAPTER THREE

EVEN in the morning there had been no ripple of news. Sam Rowan had not been early in the market but Billy White had been there. Billy grew tired of the market; prices were poor and it was a mean, drizzly day that made the world feel its old age, and made the lives of things in it the off-shoots of old age. Other farmers might have to sell, for grass was short, but there was no reason why Billy should remain nibbling at buyers; he had grass for the stock. So he whisked them out of the market, and sent them off in the care of a servant man from his neighbourhood. Billy would take a walk round and see the market, and call at Dan Sweeney's too, and have a drink; whiskey was made for such a day as this.

He pushed his way through the fair, wedging cattle aside here and there with a jerk of his thigh. A sale was taking place down near the Bank, and a big, interested crowd hung around; like crows round a stook of oats, Billy thought, spat out, and went on his way. He pushed open the door and entered Sweeney's bar. Inside, the air was thick with smoke and fumes and talk; the talk buzzed in a fog. Billy's stubble jaws felt their way among faces to the counter, and again he used his thighs to wedge obstacles aside, and a man cursed. Sweeney nodded to Billy, and filled out a double Scotch. Without a word Billy swallowed it down, and rapped the glass on the counter before Sweeney, who refilled it.

Billy rested his elbow on the counter and looked round. Talk, talk, a milling of words; here and there a song wriggled its way amid the confusion. Angry words stabbed the babel, clung on the whirl of heedlessness and hilarity, and then melted down into maudlin murmurs. Billy gazed round him; his small eyes that showed little white, blank, uninterested, just seeing, his head jerking round and round on his neck as his gaze swung.

The bar door came in with a bang, and the noise nipped off suddenly. Two men continued to drone a song until their singing stood naked amid the silence, and then they sat down suddenly, spilling their beer over each other, laughing foolishly.

'Godfrey Dhu is buying the whole damn fair,' a man roared from the doorway.

Billy White struck his glass with his elbow and it spilled across the counter, emptying over into one of his boots. His head jerked forward towards the speaker, and then crouched, as though ducking a blow, between humped shoulders. He shot out his thigh, and a man stumbled; he dug into the crowd.

'Then by God it's true!' a voice gasped close to Billy's ear.

'What's true?' Billy barked.

'The Godfrey Dhus have bought Montgomerys.'

Billy White made a noise like an animal in pain, and stood stiff against the counter. 'The Godfrey Dhus, the Godfrey Dhus.' Recollection of The Knife and Nuala and the old man himself busy among the trees was rising in gusts of alarm in Billy White, until amid the roar he accepted in a riot of rage the truth of this news. He drove his fist into the roar around him, and found a man's face, and he was in the midst of the first group that was retched out of the bar in the great heave that tore the splintered door from its hinges.

The fair was leaping into rising billows of conflict and excitement. The servant men of the Lagan were building on the gathering down near the Bank, and the Orangemen, recognising each other across spaces in the emptying market-place, moved into knots among the cattle, and then churning together drew near the roaring natives. The Godfrey Dhus were in front, silent beside a cart, with the servant men of the Lagan piled in behind them.

Billy White raced towards the Godfrey Dhus. He ran forward with an awkward jog, one clawed hand raised above his bare head, sweat beaded on his face, and blood from a cut lip dripping off his short whisker. He came on steadily, his jog settling into a purposeful stride with its queer swing. His eyes were on the old man, and when The Knife stepped forward Billy halted. Behind him the farmers of the Lagan pressed steadily, silent, this news groping into the forefront of each mind, flashing, whirling, until the fair became unreal, bizarre.

'Godfrey Dhu,' Billy White bellowed, but the servant men of the Lagan roared him down.

Breslin pushed out in front and stood a pace before Godfrey Dhu, glowering at Billy White; two enemies of a score of years. The Knife put a hand on Breslin's shoulder, and Sam Rowan walked to the front among the Orangemen. When The Knife raised his hand the market was silent.

'Is it true, Knife?'

'It's true, Sam.' And now a roar that was all challenge, the flinging of hats and of old threadbare caps: among the Orangemen a growl, here and there the sudden raising of a stick.

That scene burned deep into the minds of the Lagan. On one side the planter farmers, a solid crush of swarthy, big-bodied, well-coated men; opposing them the servant men of the Lagan, blue and grey eyes against shades of brown; fair skin against tawny, restless swaying bodies poised to spring, against a wall of stolid trunks. In front of the farmers, his small eyes blood-shot, his teeth bare, his jaws champing, his short legs wide apart, one hand clenched and held low, one raised and clawed, stood Billy White the Orangeman.

Blazing into Billy's eyes, his face thrust forward, his lips parted in a sneer, his fists pushed down along his sides by arms as stiff as ramrods, his knees bent to spring, stood Paddy Breslin, the Hibernian. Should these crowds clash, Billy and Paddy would meet first, Paddy with milling fist and butting head crashing into Billy's swinging boot and clawing hand.

Godfrey Dhu, nursing his secret of money from a dead brother's estate in Australia, had come into possession of a farm in the Lagan. Land in a compact planter district had always been disposed of by private treaty to British stock; it was part of the Orangemen's religion that the possession of soil must remain solid. This farm had passed to an absentee, and by some obscure process the absentee had let it slip into the hands of a Fenian, a papist; every native was both. Here in the market the crust of the centuries was burst; the past was boiling over, gushing out its lava of madness. Dazed, mystified, and angrier because of the mystery, the planters staggered under an eruption of boiling race hatred. One long, wild roar was ringing through the square from the servant men. Low growls from the sweating, compact, motionless Orangemen. Breslin and White, cheering and champing, straining forward. Should they meet this village will become a pit in a jungle of blind passion and men will rip one another to pieces.

Suddenly from among the natives a hand shot up commanding silence, and The Knife turned to the crowd behind him. Sam Rowan stepped to the front amid the Orangemen. His eye and The Knife's met, clear, hard looks, preoccupied; the concern of each was back on his own crowd. The Orangemen tramped past, slowly, without a word, with heavy, stamping feet. The natives were alone.

And Sam Rowan went home with the tidings which had preceded him to the fireside of the Black Rowans.

CHAPTER FOUR

NUALA GODFREY DHU was alone in the big house among the trees, and she sang as she worked in the kitchen. Being alone in this big house was an adventure, and her song was partly a challenge to the loneliness. The little cottage on the far-away slope of the hill had been without spaces, but here there was a sense of emptiness and silences. She stood by the dresser with a pile of delf in her arms and listened: the logs crackled in the wide fireplace, and, outside, beads of water plopped on a sheet of zinc under the trees. She put the delf in their place, and wondered what woman of the Montgomerys had arranged the delf in the kitchen; a quiet picturing that was sympathetic towards that wayward family. The Montgomerys were not popular among their stock; one of their breed had fought with the Americans in the War of Independence, and he had a place in history, but in the Lagan his name was only used to mock his folk. Thought of that rebel strain made the house friendly to Nuala: it took the emptiness out of the spaces.

'I'm going to like this place,' she thought, touching a plate into its place with her quick fingers.

She went upstairs to her room. Hugh and The Knife had cut down branches and now her window looked out over the broad fields, and in the distance the mountains, with shortened necks humped in the rain, cowered under leaking clouds. She smiled across at them; they reminded her, somehow, of little boys herding in the rain. She sang softly to herself as she worked, and her song now had no challenge.

It was when she was back in the kitchen that she grew restless. She went to the door, and looked out; the sky had cleared, but it was raw and she made a face at it. She went into her father's bedroom. She was still in there when she heard a shout; she paused for a moment in the bedroom door; it came again and she hurried out. She halted in the doorway, and frowned slightly. A man was coming across the open lawn; in the sunless light his face was without colour, and his hair curled on his forehead. He waved his cap to her. She stepped back into the kitchen and she was standing very erect when he came in.

'The whole fair went in a rage,' he said.

'Where's our folk?' she asked sharply.

'Comin', and half the countryside with them.'

She smiled at him now, and he came close; a whiff of whiskey came to her. 'You promised you'd stop it, James Burns,' she said.

'I'll do anything you ask me, Nuala,' he said: 'anything, but don't be a damned nun . . .'

The crash of a melodeon and voices sounded outside, and The Knife raced into the kitchen. His excitement passed at once to Nuala, and she grabbed him. They danced on to the street. Curran was singing:

'Ould Ireland will be free from the centre to the sea,
Then hurray for liberty, says the Shan Van Vocht.'

Breslin was in front, his cap on a pitchfork. Godfrey Dhu, his coat thrown across his arm, his short legs making time with the best of them, came behind Breslin.

'Then hurray for liberty, says the Shan Van Vocht,'

and the singing ended in a cheer. There were girls among the crowd, and at sight of The Knife and Nuala men grabbed them. A spurt of dancing shaped itself into an eight-hand reel. Whoops rang out, and the roll of a drum joined in the whirl of sound, for the band instruments were being carried over to Godfrey Dhu's.

'And the Orange will decay, says the Shan Van Vocht.'

Godfrey Dhu signalled The Knife and Nuala aside. 'We must get something in; we must make a night of this.'

'You old codger,' Nuala said, 'I know what's in your mind. From this day on you'll have another big day to celebrate each year.'

'I never thought to be as worked up again about anything,' he said seriously. 'I'd paste a regiment of soldiers that'd look crooked at me this minute; I'm remembering things you children never knew. Let there be such a burst of noise and laughing and roaring as will crack the panes in every damn window of their's in the Lagan.' He shook his fist towards the lights in the plain. 'Childer, if She was only living for this day,' he added after a pause. 'And you will put word to Phil Burns and Denis Freel?'

'You'll go, Knife,' Nuala said.

He nodded.

He took his bicycle and set off leisurely and then suddenly he jerked down between the handle bars and cycled for all he could.

'And the Orange will decay, says the Shan Van Vocht,' buzzed in his mind.

CHAPTER FIVE

THE bonfire at Montgomerys' gate was seen all over the Lagan. Phil Burns coming out of the byre after foddering the cows saw it, and halted for a minute to puzzle over it. Denis Freel called down to him from the roadway, and they stood side by side to wonder at it. Molly Burns came out to join them, and Denis' wife called to them from her kitchen doorway.

'It's something Carson's done,' Molly Burns said. 'For it's nothing else would get a fire under Black Rowan's nose.'

'Most like,' Denis Freel agreed.

'It's a big fire, out and out,' Phil Burns said. 'Not much sense in making fires,' he decided. 'We're as bad as themselves puttin' heed in what's most likely children's work.'

'They'd be ould-fashioned children would do yon,' Molly said, following Phil in home.

The Burns homestead was at the edge of the Lagan. The mountains ran their toes into the fields, but the Lagan itself let life flow into the crops. The Burns were a rising family: Father John was the curate in the parish below; Molly could see the smoke rise out of his house from her own doorway, and all the neighbours allowed that that was a great comfort to her. James Burns was likely to get a iob through

Father John's influence; Mary was gone off as housekeeper to her brother; a fixed situation, like marrying a stationmaster or the like, Molly said. The others of the Burnses were pressing forward in full promise, and the girls were already getting a new standing among their neighbours. Shelia was as good as engaged to Red Farrell, the publican, so that there was every sign that the family would rise clear of the bogs. Molly was considered by the neighbour women to be a " wee bit uplifted' since Father John's ordination; she now wore her boots about the house in the summer time.

Breslin burst into Burns' with the news that Godfrey Dhu had bought Montgomerys, and that the whole country was gathering there; Godfrey Dhu had sent special word to Phil Burns and Denis Freel. Denis came in, for Breslin had blurted out his story there and run on, while Phil was still listening to Breslin.

'Tie on ye, Phil,' Denis urged, 'and we'll go down; there's not a man in the world I'd be gladder to hear good of than Godfrey Dhu.'

'It will be Brian that's dead,' Phil Burns said, getting slowly to his feet. 'It would be from Brian the money came.'

'Every chance it's Brian,' Denis Freel said.

'Many a day it crossed me mind that the like of it would happen: Brian was wild, and I'm not going to deny it on him, but it's it was the wildness that ye'd like. Man alive, I must hear what happened to poor Brian: may he rest in peace.'

'You an' him were great friends sure enough,' Denis Freel said.

'He never wrote to me since we parted in Ballarat: but he was no man with a pen anyway. But truer chum a man never stepped out with.'

Phil had his stick in his hand now.

'I saw us one day in the bush . . .' Denis Freel and Phil Burns were off down the road, Phil telling stories of his Australian days.

Molly stood in the doorway; voices were calling here and there and fires were blazing on all the spots where they had blazed when elections were won.

'People lose their heads for nothing,' she grumbled.

Sally Freel came dandering in. 'I suppose like myself your toes are broke outside gaping at the fires.'

'Indeed no, for I was busy: I'm knitting a pair of gloves for Father John, and it takes the light for the fine yarn.'

'The Godfrey Dhus is getting cheered the night if ever there was a family cheered; you'd think it's Home Rule the people'd got. They'll be at the head of the Lagan after this,' Sally said.

'It's the fair and a fit of foolishness,' Molly suggested.

'Dan Sweeney is in the back seat the night,' Sally persisted. 'He was left with an empty shop; the whole fair emptied out to Montgomery's. It's kind of hard on Dan Sweeney that always used to have the crowds himself; the Godfrey Dhus that was only hard-workin' men yesterday leadin' the Lagan the day.'

'When it comes to leadin' the Lagan, people'll have to look to wiser heads than the Godfrey Dhus,' Molly said.

'It's funny: a man like Dan Sweeney builds and builds and spends years at it, and then up shoots the Godfrey Dhus and he's left high and dry. One day you think you see a family risin' up big before their neighbours, and the next thing is some other family leaps up half-way to the sky. The way people is looking up to the Godfrey Dhus all of a sudden would stagger ye. I must run, for I left a pot on the fire,' Sally said.

'There never comes a word out of your lips but has a bite against this family in it,' Molly muttered. 'Devil all Phil's but an ould fool anyway,' she grumbled. 'Godfrey Dhus lead the Lagan, moryah,' she thought, looking at Father John's photo with the lamp shining on it.

CHAPTER SIX

IT was true enough for Sally Freel, Dan Sweeney had been deserted by the crowd for once. He watched the fair march out of the town, and was suddenly alarmed. His alarm broke down, however, under more reasoned consideration. The band were Hibernians to a man, and the bulk of them were more or less in his books; likely as not scores of them would be in trouble with the police before morning, and they would be coming to him to make things easy for them. Dan's power was well based. He was chairman of the Hibernians, a magistrate, post-master, secretary to the old age pension committee, and the biggest merchant in the town; the public house was in his wife's name. 'I could whistle the crowd to heel,' he thought, but he went slowly upstairs to his den.

He buried himself deep in a chair before a crackling fire of well-seasoned chunks of bog fir; yes, he was worried, and he had reason. The news that had rocked the bar and split the fair had come without warning; the like of that had never happened in the Lagan before. Events had always followed Dan's knowledge of their coming, and of the causes working to produce them. Here was a family so deep and strong that it kept a big scheme within itself until the event was born. Such minds could not help but challenge some of Dan's power; already they had jeopardised some of his plans.

Had there been anybody in the secret with the Godfrey Dhus? It would have been a relief, in a way, to know that Father Burns or old Father Coll was in this thing with them; it would make them smaller folk in Dan's eyes. Father Burns: Dan called him forward again before his mind to review his judgment of him: fussy, self-important, conceited, good little man; like a clucking hen on the look for worms for her chicks, he was eyeing round for jobs for his family, and was now depending on Dan to get the Rate Collectorship for his brother James. No danger in a man like that. Dan's power had grown because he had never pushed a relation for anything; family pushers narrow in their base and topple sideways. No, Father Burns was a useful little man with no opening into influence, except such opening as Dan would give.

Father Coll? No, he would have heard through the housekeeper. No, damn them, it was a deep, strong decision, reared in the family without a word, and put on its feet without a stagger.

Light footsteps sounded in the corridor.

'Nora!' Dan Sweeney called, 'Nora!'

A black, curly-haired girl pushed her head in the door. 'Were you calling, father?'

'Was I roaring. Come here.' The girl came rapidly across the room. 'Isn't that ginger snap that tomboys around with you one of the Godfrey Dhus?'

'Nuala; you know her fine. She cycled to the convent every morning when I was there.'

'Fat lot you did.'

'Well, she did; all the Godfrey Dhus have brains.'

'Did you know about them buying this farm?'

'I knew about the money.'

'And, you strap, you never told me,' he roared, turning round to face her.

'It was a secret, father.'

'Come over here till I see you right. Who the devil do you take after? Damned if I know.' But he smiled at her, for the Godfrey Dhus had suddenly become less formidable; his old strings could yet hold the Lagan, there was no danger to his rule. 'Have you that list ready for me?' he asked abruptly.

The girl's face hardened suddenly. 'I have, and, father, I wish I hadn't to help you in that way.'

'What way? Is it too much to make out a list of the poor folk that are looking for pensions?'

'But you will go out now to these folk and promise them their books in a day or two, and they'll get them. And poor old Betty Nelly gave me five shillings out of her first pension to get a mass said for you. I hate things like that.'

Dan Sweeney's eyes were hard. 'Sit down,' he said.

His daughter sat in a chair opposite. 'You don't go sayin' these things all over the place?'

'I'm too ashamed to do anything of the sort.'

'How do you think everything came our way – post office and everything? You must have power if you're going to get things.'

'And I wonder why you and Father Burns are backing the volunteers and I be afraid.'

'Aren't we Irishmen as good Irishmen as any in the county?' he demanded, sitting up in his chair.

'Father Burns changed his talk after you went to see him.'

'Isn't that to my credit?'

'The Knife is puzzled.'

'And who is The Knife?'

'Brian Godfrey Dhu.'

'And he is puzzled. Damn his skin, what concern is it of his?'

'He's a volunteer.'

'James Burns is in charge of the volunteers.'

'James is anything Nuala wants him to be.'

'By God!' Dan Sweeney gasped, and sat back in his chair. 'Why in heaven's name didn't you tell me this before?'

'I'm not sure I should have told it at all.' She got to her feet and came to his side.

'Father,' she said softly.

'Well?'

'You are not . . .?'

'Not what?'

'Earning a post office or the like?'

'I am just doing what's right for the country. Honest to God,' he added, after a pause. And then with an impatient grunt he waved his daughter out of the room.

CHAPTER SEVEN

Billy White's farm touched Montgomerys on one side, and for years his cattle had had the run of the two holdings. It was like losing a part of his farm to have the fence put in repair. Each morning he hurried down through the trees to discover whether work had begun; and the day came when he heard the ring of an axe chopping wood. He stole cautiously to the fringe of the trees. Breslin was driving paling stabs preparing for wiring. Billy gave his short squeal like an animal in pain. He champed his jaws and seized a dead branch and snapped it between his hands; he dug into the soil with his heels, his vision of Breslin blurred. He darted suddenly from the cover of the trees and came close, his small, restless eyes blazing.

Breslin's face darkened, and his eyes flamed like Billy's. He opened his mouth in a mocking laugh, showing his long, scattered, yellow teeth.

'Good morning, Mr. White,' he greeted with mock formality.

Billy went on champing his jaws; Breslin's dog growled.

'Don't be angry now,' Breslin said to the dog. 'He's only a poor ignorant runt of an Orange bastard.' He took up his stab and walked towards

Billy. He put the point of it in the ground and struck. Billy squealed and jumped towards Breslin; that stab hurt as though it had entered his foot; it was on Billy's land. They stood jammed close together, their bodies taut, their eyes on a level. Breslin's hand tightened on the haft of the axe. Neither spoke; and when they heard sounds, steps, neither moved nor looked. The Knife had come to help Breslin put up the fence and Sam Rowan had come down after Billy White. Sam had been looking on for some minutes. The Knife and he exchanged looks, cold, hard looks without hate or friendliness.

'Drop the hatchet,' The Knife said.

Both men started and drew apart; they glowered in silence.

'That stab is too far out, Breslin,' The Knife said quietly.

Sam Rowan nodded and then signalled Billy and withdrew.

'Ye see now what am puttin' up wi',' Billy White pleaded. 'Stealin' me land.' Sam walked in silence. Billy grew sullen in the silence and he glanced uneasily at Sam Rowan.

'Breslin's provokin',' Sam said at last. 'The Knife would nae let him.'

'He would nae? Feart; just feart.'

'The Knife feart, Billy?' Sam shook his head. 'Man, he's nae feart.'

'I know what brought ye now,' Billy growled. 'You heard?'

'I heard, and it's not going to happen,' Sam said.

'Who hell'll stop it?'

'I'll stop it, till other folks have their say.'

'An' for why, for why would you try to stop it,' Billy pleaded.

'If ye burn Montgomerys where'll it end? The whole Lagan'll roast; them that has least can burn most.'

'An' is it leave them here to root and breed? Roast them now before they spread over the place like whins.'

'I'll just tell the police and let them guard it.'

Billy White stood aghast. 'You'd never do that, Sammy, give them a guard like a judge.'

'I'll just do that, Billy.'

They stood facing each other in anger among the trees.

'An' what is it now I am to promise not to do?'

'You're to give up the notion of burning Montgomerys.'

Billy was silent; his small dark eyes were on the ground, his head moving round in jerks as he glanced about him where he stood. He threw back his head and flashed his eyes at Sam, hovering on the edge of violent repudiation of Sam's authority. The clear, brown, cold eyes above absorbed Billy's look and beat it down as a searchlight might eat up a flare. Billy stamped about and grumbled, low, plaintive grumbles. And then suddenly he was silent; he stood very still; the restless jerking of his head stopped.

'I'll promise you I'll not burn Montgomerys,' he said, without looking up. 'Damn ye, Sam Rowan, I promise ye.' A weasel shot out from the old fence and Billy dived for stones which he flung with terrific force. He toppled the weasel and raced down on the wounded animal, raining missiles as he ran.

Sam Rowan gazed at him for a while; then slowly he nodded to himself and turned away.

CHAPTER EIGHT

'WE are just as anxious to save them from violence as we are to get them out of Montgomery's; violence spreads, and they might spread. We are against both.'

'Any violence now would be like to spread,' Dan Sweeney said, seriously.

'Violence is to be avoided at all costs,' Father Burns said, and the two Orangemen nodded.

The little conference was being held in the bank, the Orangemen had asked for it. The purpose was to arrive at a bargain with the Godfrey Dhus when they would vacate Montgomerys.

'The terms you offer are good terms,' Father Burns continued, 'and they may consider themselves well treated.'

'We just want peace in the Lagan,' the Orangemen said. 'It was madness of them to leap in bare-handed among bayonets.'

'I have always found you gentlemen reasonable, and always on the side of peace,' Dan Sweeney said. 'That's why I brought Father Burns to you; it's nothing I can do.'

'We are very glad to have a neighbour's son in such high standing among us,' one of the Orangemen said.

'I will do my best for the peace of the Lagan,' Father Burns said, getting to his feet. He shook hands with the others.

'By the by, Father, now that you are here you should remind these gentlemen that James comes up for election for the rate collectorship, next council meeting.'

Father Burns blushed and was embarrassed.

'Don't worry, Father Burns,' the Orange spokesman assured him. 'There is feeling against the appointment now, I tell you frankly, but we will get over it. Only for give-and-take among the educated in the Lagan I wonder where we would all land. You will do your best, Father?'

'I don't like promising, but I feel sure — '

'We are perfectly satisfied, Father, perfectly satisfied. You can tell James from us that he has that appointment.'

Dan Sweeney put his arm through Father Burns'. 'You made a good impression on them,' he said as soon as they were outside. 'A good impression, Father. I was proud of ye myself; cautious; nothing impresses them like cautious talk.'

'They made it look too much like a bargain,' Father Burns grumbled.

'Well, as they say, without give-and-take among the leaders where would we be?'

A countryman approached the priest to go on a sick call, and he hurried away on his bicycle.

And that evening he called on the Godfrey Dhus. Coming up the avenue he noticed the old man going in among the trees with an axe, and he followed him. Godfrey Dhu waited for him resting the axe on the trunk of a fallen tree. As the priest drew near he took a few steps forward with his hand out.

'I'm glad to welcome you to Montgomerys,' Godfrey Dhu said.

'I was anxious to get to see you as soon as I could; my father often talked about your family,' Father Burns responded.

'About Brian he talks always,' Godfrey Dhu said. 'You'll come inside? Nuala is wanting you to say mass in the house as soon as you can: I was saying it's a station you should give out in it: it would drive half the Lagan mad.'

'It's not a very good reason for a station,' Father Burns said coldly.

Godfrey Dhu thought it over for a few minutes and was unrepentant. ''Deed be me soul is it,' he persisted.

'Driving the Lagan mad is not a thing that would do much good. I don't mind telling you, Godfrey Dhu, that though you may have done yourself a good turn in buying this place, you don't help the country.'

'That's not a notion I can see much sense in,' Godfrey Dhu said.

'It's hard enough to keep Carson's volunteers and our own quiet when it's only ideas is in their minds, but when the Orangemen see you coming in on their land they will see a target.'

'Coming in on their land. Your notion is easier to see now, and it has quare roots. Did you ask your father his idea?'

Father Burns cut at a fern with his stick.

'They're leppin' mad, the whole damn lot of them,' Godfrey Dhu chuckled.

'The task of keeping the Lagan quiet doesn't fall on you, Godfrey Dhu.'

'It does not fall on me,' Godfrey Dhu agreed. 'It does not fall on me.'

'Your father has as nice a crop of spuds the year as ever I saw,' Godfrey Dhu resumed after a pause. 'I was down in your house yesterday: I was over with a load of spuds to Denis Freel. Your mother is as young looking as she was twenty years ago. Ye're a great man, we're all proud of ye, Father Burns, for I hear ye were the smartest man they ever had in the college; but you'll be a great man if them you are on a level with think as much of you as his neighbours think of your father.'

Father Burns felt suddenly uncomfortable; they were near the edge of the trees and had only a strip of green to cross to reach the open door.

'Listen to me, Godfrey Dhu,' Father Burns said. 'I'm worried about your coming here: the Ulster volunteers look on it as a challenge to them, and with all this excitement things could happen easily. Would you not take a profit and leave Montgomerys and go into some business? Dan Sweeney says you could set up in business in some of the towns in the back country on half what you paid for this farm.'

'Dan wouldn't like us to go into the town beyond?'

'He was very fair about that: he says they're always owin' him more or less, and that they'd stick to him on that account, and that the ones that would run to you would be the ones he wouldn't give credit to, folk that would be a burden to any business man.'

'An' wouldn't it be the same in any other town?'

'Well, in the back country there's not such a struggle between Catholics' and Protestants' shops, and there would be no good in you and Dan starting a fight for it's our own people you'd be dividing between you.'

Godfrey Dhu opened his mouth and laughed silently. 'Did you ever ask your father what him and me thinks of Dan Sweeney?' he asked.

'My father and you may have old-fashioned good sense, but you are poor judges of what is right for you to-day.'

'Is it me and Phil Burns wouldn't know what's good for the Lagan? You may be smart, and very smart, Father John, an' I be proud when I hear it said how smart ye are, but they have nothin' in the books about the Lagan because Phil Burns an' me and Denis Freel never wrote no book about the Lagan.'

Father Burns made a gesture of impatience.

'And as for Dan Sweeney, he never grew a thought yet that wasn't full up of meanin' for himself; the most harmless word ever he says to a man has a meanin' in it. And Dan Sweeney has a meanin' in tryin' to get us out: an' holy men is the least people that has a chance with Dan Sweeney. Some bargain he's makin' with the Orangemen.'

'Do you think I'd make a bargain with the Orangemen,' Father Burns stormed.

'If you were to do anything of the kind, you would be no son of Phil Burns, but mind that Dan Sweeney doesn't lead you into his schemes.'

'If I didn't know you were my father's friend I'd be very angry,' Father Burns said.

'I'm your father's friend,' Godfrey Dhu said. 'There's truth in every word of that.'

'Then won't you let me advise you?'

'I'll hear any advice you have to give.'

'I ask you then to take a good profit for your farm and sell it.'

'Tell Dan Sweeney from me that I bought this farm knowing what I was doing, and praying to put the whole Lagan leppin' mad, and that if I am spoilin' some wee scheme of his then I'll be gladder and gladder I bought it.'

'Do you think I am a penny boy for Dan Sweeney?' Father Burns said angrily.

'You wouldn't be a son of your father if you were. Come in, and Nuala will make you a cup of tea.'

But Father Burns was in a hurry, and went back to his bicycle; Godfrey Dhu returned to his axe, and began vigorously to chop a fallen tree.

CHAPTER NINE

DOCTOR HENRY came back from a few days' visit to the city, and called at Rowans on his way home. When Rebecca saw his car stop she knew that he was unlikely to have heard the news about Montgomerys, and having to tell it deepened her gloom. Doctor Henry came striding in in his lazy, long-legged way, and drew a chair towards the fire before he became aware of the unusual atmosphere.

'What at all's wrong with you all?' he asked, pausing with the chair resting on two legs.

'There's plenty wrong wi' us,' Rebecca said shortly.

'Aye? It's no Sam?' he asked.

'Na, it's no Sam,' William said. And just then Sam came in from the yard.

'What cloud is on ye all?' the Doctor asked.

'The Godfrey Dhus have bought Montgomery's place,' Sam said.

The Doctor whistled, drew forward his chair, and sat down. 'Well, the like of it had to happen,' he said, lighting a strip of paper. 'It had to come. With them folk rising up like braird all round ye, and becoming people of standing here and there, it just had to come. It would be foolish to fash yourselves about what is natural.'

'That's strange talk,' Rebecca said. 'An' it's talk that's no to me likin'.'

'An' it's the Godfrey Dhus bought it: a stubborn, stiff-necked breed the men, and a skinful of dynamite the woman,' Doctor Henry mused.

'What's going to be done about it?' Rebecca asked, getting to her feet. 'Is it sittin' sayin' things to one another ye are when every teachin' ye ever heard is going to pieces: if a papish family gets in on the land the servant men of the Lagan will be fair walkin' on people in a month.'

'When servant men begin to walk on folk, they'll have a kick at papists and Orangemen alike,' the Doctor said, new home from an industrial England.

'There's goin' to be blood spilt over this; there'll be plottin' and thinkin' and plannin' and the bad drop will break out in them. An' Home Rule behind it all,' she concluded.

'It's goin' to be a quare prickly bed for the Godfrey Dhus,' the Doctor said. 'Couldn't they be got to get out of it?' he added thoughtfully, turning towards Sam.

Rebecca paused with a bowl in her hand, halting while about to rest it on a shelf.

'It would take a lot to shift them,' Sam said. 'Still, if a body tried to do it he would be a better judge; it's a guy ticklish thing,' he added.

There was silence for a while in the kitchen; and then the Doctor went slowly back to his car. Sam saw him down to the pass.

'The Knife is one a body can have a thing out with, anyway,' the Doctor said. 'I'm afraid there'll be trouble.'

'It's just touch and go; and I think Father Burns an make little of them.'

'He'd make little of them,' Doctor Henry agreed.

When he arrived at Montgomerys, Nuala chanced to be alone in the kitchen. She was flattening out a scone of oaten bread on the kitchen table. The Doctor rested a hand on the top of the door and leaned cross-legged against the edge.

'I'll bet you a shilling you break it,' he said.

Nuala ran her hand under the wide, thin, circular, highly brittle cake, and raised it, and then revolving it round and round between her palms she brought it unbroken to the fire and stood it against the bread iron. Her face was flushed with the excitement of it, for she had been wondering whether she was capable of such a feat with so large sized a cake when the Doctor arrived. She turned with outstretched hand towards him, and he laid his shilling in her palm.

'I'll keep it for luck,' she said, blowing on it.

'You're recruited to the Orangemen now,' the Doctor said.

'Then you have your work before you to make them accept the recruit,' she challenged.

'Ye have the truth there,' the Doctor said gravely, 'and I may as well say straight out I think it was looking for trouble to come here: not but you have a right to come in,' he added.

'That's a big admission,' Nuala said. 'Won't you sit up and we will argue about it. Now tell me what the Orangemen are saying?' She was in dead earnest behind her banter, for she felt that only excited talk could have driven any Orangeman to such a step as this.

'Let me try to make a speech,' the Doctor said with a smile. 'Now first of all I'm only a poor sort of Orangeman – my while in England kind of made an Irishman of me. It's only at home an Orangeman is not Irish; in England he'd beat the face off anybody who insisted he was English. I'm against all this fuss and talk and drill and all the Carson nonsense: it is just a big show off. But down here on the Lagan some think Home Rule is a bit of heaven with all the priests for it, and more think it's a bit of hell with all the ministers against it, and between them they just keep Orangemen and Catholics ready to burn one another. When all this bad feeling is there, any wee thing can set it rioting, and I'm afraid your coming here will do it. An' I'd be terrible sorry if it made worse trouble between folk, for once a blow is struck it travels.'

'An' you're not against Home Rule?' Nuala asked, in some amazement.

'In a way I am; and in a way I'm not. It's not fair to keep all the jobs for Orangemen; but we have them, and we're loth to let go and give them to an Irish parliament to share out; we'd get very few, maybe.'

'But it's freedom the people want, not just the jobs, Doctor Henry,' Nuala protested.

'Well now yon's what we are against, Nuala, losing all the power of patronage and all that; so it must be what your side is after, I'm thinking.'

'An' why should not our men have good jobs in their own country?'

'It's just because I say the same that I'm against all this fighting; let's share and share. In the long run it's likely that we'll be out of parliament, but the fellows that go in are not going to be so well-to-do but they'll be open to be influenced this way and that; it's not like as if the fight were about something big, it's just a scramble, that's all it is.'

'A body sees your mind; it's a damp, boggy kind of mind.'

'My mind has just as much spring in it as anybody's mind,' the Doctor said. 'It's what I see I'm talking about, not what I am. I see that you've a right to be here; I see that it's maybe going to be cruel for you if you stay here. Does saying that and seeing that make me be thought of as against you?'

Nuala got to her feet. The sun through the window glistened in her hair, and her face glowed underneath. 'So you have come to warn us, you too, Doctor Henry.'

'Me too?' the Doctor asked.

'Aye, Father Burns was at it already.'

'So you won't go?'

'We just won't go.'

'Well maybe you'd let me welcome you to Montgomery's. I'm likely to be the only Orangeman will do it.'

He shook hands and without further remark went out. Nuala watched him disappear down the path.

CHAPTER TEN

NORA DAN SWEENEY burst into Nuala's room. It was evening and the trees were a brown bank, except where a new moon strained through the tips of a few branches; Nuala was at the window looking out.

Nora dashed over to her and hugged her with gusto.

'It's just great,' she said. 'It's just great.' And then, 'Nuala Godfrey Dhu, you of all the world crying.'

'I don't know, Nora, but it's different somehow; people are going to be different too.'

'Tell the wise woman of the Lagan your sorrows,' Nora urged, relieved to find that no bad news had come to Nuala.

Nuala's face shone in a ribbon of starlight and she smiled.

'Now don't get away up in one of your white moods among the stars,' Nora pleaded. 'You frighten me then. Do you mind the nights up in the tower in Aileach? I'm not a bit surprised poor father is worried about you.'

'Your father?'

'Aye; I left him and Father Burns about chokin'. James Burns backed me up fine. Do you know,

Nuala, he's making a new man of himself since yon night of the raffle at Aileach.'

Nuala was silent.

'So long as he thinks he's making a fine fellow of himself in your eyes he'll go on and on. But I wouldn't like you to marry him, Nuala; he's not the kind of man was to sweep in from the mountain and free the country and marry you.'

'What worried your father?'

'He was tellin' James that the Lagan couldn't last a night if the Orangemen thought guns were comin' into it, and that the rifles that were under the stage in the Hibernian Hall must be taken up at once and built into father's counter. Before James could say a word I laughed.

' "You go to Nuala and tell her that," I said, making a great joke of it.

' "What the hell has she to do with it?"

' "Maybe I shouldn't have told you at all?" I said, looking at Burns and pretending to be in a swither.

' "What in God's name do you mean?" he roared.

' "Sure Nuala has the guns stored in Montgomerys this long time," I said.

'My father leapt round at James. "It's not true," he gasped, and sure enough James rose to it like a man.

' "What's wrong with it?" he challenged, as bold as you like.

'Father sat down. I never saw him deflated like that before.

' "I was always against any guns," he said. "Always. But nothing would do but we must get some to show the men. Now this woman has them. How are you going to get them back?"

'"Aren't they safe enough?" James says.

'My father is cute, he put it no further.

'"Everybody says Nuala is the woman of the prophecy, don't they, James?" I said.

'"What prophecy?"

'"A woman that was to arise in the Lagan and lead the men of Ireland. . . ."

'And then my father spluttered, "God Almighty, let a story like that make headway . . ." He jumped up and waved his arms and I winked to James and we both cleared.

'"An' the rifles?"

'"James and The Knife are away to get them brought here for fear father might take the notion to search."'

Nuala nodded and was silent.

'What was worrying you?' Nora asked, after a pause.

'It was just a mood maybe; Mary Burns was with me all the evening too.'

'Nice poor soul, Mary,' Nora said.

'Father Burns had been out with father the other day, and I could see that he was on some business, and that my father was pulling against him. It was the same business as Mary's; trying to frighten us out of Montgomerys.'

'It's not trying to frighten you made you cry, Nuala.'

'It's not.'

'Wouldn't I love to see Mary cluck-clucking round you.'

Nuala smiled. 'Mary says we made a mistake anyway at the very beginning, that it's an invitation party we had a right to give instead of letting the Lagan pour in on top of us.'

'They did that,' Nora said, 'and Sally Freel wasn't asked till the last minute, and she has a pick at them ever since.'

'Mary says we'll never get the standing we should among the neighbours once we made a mistake at the start, and she says that if we opened a business in a strange town Father Burns and your father would help us in any way they could.'

Nora Dan Sweeney laughed and flung herself down on Nuala's bed.

'And this evening the boys at the gate said, "Good evening, miss," and touched their caps,' Nuala added.

'So that's why you were feeling lonely,' Nora said quietly. 'Workin' chaps is like that, afraid of a girl that has finer clothes than their own womenfolk, and some cheap Johnnie that's like a scalded cat would have the neck of the devil.'

They both laughed, and were silent for a while.

'You think it's me is making James Burns work, Nora; well, you're wrong. He's just in earnest in what he's doing.'

'I'm courtin' on and off since I was sixteen, Nuala, and have me good three years' experience; you're green crops compared to me, for all your extra three months.'

'Fat lot you know about it,' Nuala scoffed.

A burst of whistling sounded outside.

'That's The Knife,' Nora said, flinging out of the bed.

'And the rifles,' Nuala said, bounding to her feet too.

And down below in the darkness the four young people chuckled now and then as they arranged a hiding-place for the rifles. And on the way back The Knife and Nora got separated from Nuala and James Burns.

CHAPTER ELEVEN

THE Godfrey Dhus noticed that their nods were not returned by the neighbour farmers, and soon meetings went without greeting from either side. So that when The Knife went into the market to buy young beasts to put on the grass, he was more or less prepared for his reception. He first met Billy White, who had two bullocks for sale.

'What'll ye take for them, Billy?' The Knife asked. Billy was sitting on the side of a cart.

'I want nothing from you,' Billy said without looking at him.

The Knife strode leisurely up to Billy. 'So ye want nothing from me, Billy?' he said.

'They're sold,' Billy said, dropping to his feet.

After a short pause, The Knife walked away. He rapped many beasts but made no purchase. In the throng he came face to face with Sam Rowan.

'Have ye sold your beasts, Sam?' he asked. 'I like that wee polly.'

Sam hesitated. Then he looked at The Knife squarely. 'To tell you the truth, Knife, am no' sellin' anything to ye.'

'I'm in the market this couple of hours, Sam,' The Knife said, 'and to tell you the truth, I wouldn't take a present of most of the beasts I priced. I was in earnest with you. An' yer the only Orangeman in the fair I didn't make a liar of.'

'A liar?'

The Knife nodded. 'There's Bob Weldon. He asked me fourteen pounds for that wee bullock. Isn't that a plain lie to say that's his price?'

Weldon heard him, as it was intended he should. 'I wouldn't take fourteen pounds of yer bloody money: there's no knowing how ye got it,' he retorted.

'Where's your Dick?' The Knife asked sharply.

'He's around the market. What ye want wi' Dick?' he added, annoyed with himself.

'I was wonderin' could he be got to say what you said.'

'I wouldn't ask ye for yer beast now, Sam Rowan,' The Knife continued, 'for if it was that ye sold to me every one of them would be nippin' at ye, the dark-minded lot of damn fools.'

'I wouldn't let me tongue get speeded up like that, Knife,' Sam said curtly.

The Knife and Sam straightened at the same instant and faced each other. The crowds had been gradually closing in behind them, for their meeting was of significance to the whole fair. Breslin was beside The Knife. Billy White pushed forward near Sam.

'Up, Montgomery,' Breslin taunted, his eye on Billy.

The Rowans had Montgomery blood in them, and Sam struck; The Knife dodged, and crouching, struck back.

The fair was in an uproar in an instant. The

Knife and Sam hurled forward into conflict and the fair rocked under their impact. A silence swept across the market, clipping the words from ready lips, halting the bargaining hands in the air. From mind to mind, from body to body, excitement leaped in sudden heady flashes, and a hurried, restless local grouping took place all across the market, and then with a flick the groups rose tiptoe, and tipped towards the whirlpool in the centre. A roar leaped from so many throats that tired cattle pranced in affright, and then the groups linked, chained, and swung themselves round the fighters, pressing back to make space, bellowing a rage that seemed to break in adequate expression in the swirling, thumping, berserker bodies in front. Sam Rowan, suddenly lightfooted, quick-minded, headlong; The Knife, his lithe form nimble as cane, ribs like steel casing, knuckles like the teeth of a harrow, was lifted forward in a burst of madness such as never had burst in his soul. A wild, long roar; milling feet; repressed enmity suddenly ablaze. The damning years reel again under the impetus, and when they break two tidal waves will crash, and the very sun will be washed out of the blue heavens. Faster the pace between Sam and The Knife; gasps have a place in the medley; blood flows down fair and tawny skins; this is a fight that will end in one or both of these bodies sinking into the mud, as dead, as exhausted of purpose or meaning, as this missionless muck.

Police whistles have been sounding, and now a new shout, sharp, shrill, closer to action than that wild storm of sound. The police, with drawn batons, charge into the natives. The Orangemen, barricaded, leap forward. Men fall and are trampled, ribs crack under the vicious stamp of steel heel plates, sticks break across bleeding heads. Men drop under the rain of batons, the nervous whisperings of defeat melting the natives' passion. Suddenly police and Orangemen in a mighty heave fling the natives before them like a sapless crust of lost passion and the fight becomes a chase. Native Ireland was swept from the fair, and only women and children, wild-eyed, furtive, raced through the village to collect bellowing cattle and hurry them out to the little homesteads in the hills.

Sam Rowan had seen The Knife go down under the smash of a baton: then he lost vision of things. He was held erect by two stocky farmers while he gasped for breath and spat blood, and blinked sweat and blood from his eyelashes. The sharp tang of whiskey on his cut lips, the murmur of encouraging voices, the wild throatfuls of sudden cheer, these things he heard as they linked him from the field.

The Knife was taken to the police barracks.

CHAPTER TWELVE

DOCTOR HENRY from his top window had seen the fair rock under the first impact between Sam and The Knife. He groaned, kicked a chair round, and flopped into it. Nothing could save the vomit of madness now. The Doctor's chin rested in his hands, his fingers, like steel rods, pressed deep into his cheeks, he swayed gently as he sat. When the police – they were dozens in strength on fair days – swept into view, their helmets aglitter, batons swinging, he rose suddenly to his feet. He stood very still and when the crash took place he blinked. His face was ridged with the track of his fingers, and his body trembled. With an abrupt gesture he turned round and walked out of the room.

He was sitting in his study, stretched out on the sofa, gazing up at the ceiling, when his door was flung open. Nuala Godfrey Dhu was in the doorway. The Doctor flashed his eyes into hers, and waited.

'Will you insist on seeing The Knife in the barracks?' she asked. He was erect before her in an instant.

'I'll see him,' he said. 'Wait here.'

Nuala had seen most of it from Nora's room, for the police whistles had drawn them both to the windows. The first wild resistance to the police had swept the girls into the spirit of the crowd outside. With the bursting of the resistance, Nora flung her arms round Nuala and moaned. The Orangemen mixed in with the police, and their cheers rang through the town. And then a bloody, muddy form was dragged into view.

'The Knife,' Nora gasped. She took her arms from around Nuala. 'The Knife,' she said this time in a clear, ringing call. Pulling at Nuala's hand, she raced for the door.

The police would not let them near the prisoner. Nuala left Nora struggling and arguing at the barrack door, and hastened round for the Doctor. She paced his room, and waited. She suddenly discovered she was thirsty; there was a syphon on the sideboard; she squirted out a hasty drink, sipped it, and sat down on the couch from which the Doctor had risen.

She was without thought; merely toned up to some thoughtless alarm. Or was it alarm? Or pain? Or anger? She discovered she was trembling. What had she said to the Doctor? In here . . . not knowing what she had said. What had she said? 'Go to The Knife'? Had the Doctor made for Montgomerys? She got to her feet. Her trembling was less now. Her seized mind was again flexible, active.

She was sure she must have asked him to see The Knife in the barracks. She could have said nothing else. It was as though she had frozen and the only fluid thing in her body was the idea to get Doctor Henry to the barracks to The Knife. She must have said that.

Why had she not gone with the Doctor? She

should have got in with him but her mind had been numbed. She probably would have followed him without thought of staying had he not said, 'Wait here.' Of course, she had only come for the Doctor, and she had intended to go back with him. She drew in a deep breath; bells were ringing in her ear; the sound was dying. That was how she came to hear it. She was herself again now. Best thing to do was to wait.

She sat down again. Lucky the Doctor had been home. Instinctively she had come to Doctor Henry. He had been approachable to her for years; they had often met at the bedside of poor Norah Boyle. Would he wonder at her racing in like this? Anyway he would do his best; his best would be good. She smiled ever so slightly. Doctor Henry would put his heart into his work for The Knife.

So this was his room. It was just like Doctor Henry to have his books scattered. A slipper in each corner, his pipe on the carpet; she poked a burnt spot with her toe. Just like the Doctor. Pictures on the walls. Dunfanaghy Bay. Who was the woman over the mantelpiece? An old painting. She got to her feet. The face interested her, a warm face, a heavy face, there was something she did not like in that face, something in the face she did not wish for the Doctor. No photo of himself. And what was that pinned under the picture frame? A feather; a feather with a date on it; a goose feather. And then suddenly she was uneasy and stepped back from the picture. It was the feather she had given to Doctor Henry one day to pick out his pipe. She stood back from the picture; her cheeks were tinged with colour.

'So he keeps that pipe cleaner,' she said to herself. Funny thing to date it. She sat down. It was wrong to go peering round a man's room.

Her mind went back to The Knife. And now she found that her thoughts overflowed with the happenings at the fair. Strange that she had been able to miss thinking of these things. What had started it? The Knife must have been deep in at the very heart of it. Montgomery's was underneath even the heart of the happenings, and the madness of it all came from deeper and deeper. Why had the crowd broken? Why must they always break? If Knife was dead, the blame was on the running crowd. Wait till she got them together. Where had James Burns been? She placed him against the strength of the police drive. She shook her head quickly. He could not hold there. She got to her feet again. Would the Doctor never come?

A maid came in with the tea tray; Nuala drank the tea slowly. She was not yet finished when she heard the Doctor's step in the corridor and she had the door open when he reached it.

'Well?'

'Fine! You know, Nuala, it would take more than a fair day to kill The Knife. He's well bruised, but he will be all right; absolutely all right. I've made it as bad as I can to keep them from sending him to jail.'

'Who fought him, or was it the whole fair?'

'It began with one man; he's outside here. He'll tell the story as it happened anyway.'

'Will you let me hear him tell it?' Nuala asked.

The Doctor nodded, went to the door and

beckoned. Then he shut the door and put his hand to it for a second.

'Who do you think fought The Knife?'

'There's only one man would be likely to face The Knife, that's Sam Rowan.'

The Doctor opened the door and Sam Rowan came in. One eye was closed, his lip was swollen, and sticking plaster belted one eyebrow. His cheek was brown with iodine patches.

'It was a fair fight. I'm to blame,' Sam said quietly. 'I was round arguin' with them that if the police take him they should take me too.'

'And why did you and The Knife, the two most alike men in the Lagan, why did you fight?'

'We just fought, Nuala. I struck The Knife.'

'And what made you do that, Sam Rowan?' she asked earnestly, like a child that is hurt.

Sam shook his head.

'Then I'll tell you, Sam Rowan,' Nuala burst out. 'You were doin' a thing you didn't like in the market and that made you touchy; a thing you didn't like, and because you couldn't face it, you faced The Knife. Oh! Sam Rowan, Sam Rowan,' she said, standing straight before him. And then before either of the men could say anything she walked out.

CHAPTER THIRTEEN

PHIL BURNS went across to Denis Freel, and they both sat down among the turf to have a smoke. Phil held out his pouch to Denis and they got a light from the little fire that Denis kept alive.

'It's not many people keeps a couple of coals alive now to light the pipe on,' Phil commented. 'Matches, matches, all the time. I never got no good out of a match.'

'Matches and shop clothes, and I hear that there's people buy socks in the shops now. The old people give'd us a harder life than them's coming on now is gettin'. People's gettin' away more and more from the roots of their work. There's the whole Lagan through the fields an' I suppose for the one that's thinkin' on what he's doin' there's ten that's remembering the fair.'

'People's fair risen,' Phil Burns said. 'I have to tell myself twenty times a day that I'm not to be puttin' me own views on Father John and James, and in spite of it all I go up in the air now and then. It seems Dan Sweeney and them blame The Knife for the trouble at the fair.'

'There's no blackguardism in the Godfrey Dhus,' Denis Freel said.

'Is it in the Godfrey Dhus? Indeed no,' Phil

agreed. 'Us old people may as well keep our mouths shut. I'd fight Carson myself, but it's not Dan Sweeney I'd have leading me, and Father John gets mad when I say anything like that.'

'It's some wee trick of his own Dan's after,' Denis Freel said. 'Declare if that's not Godfrey Dhu himself riding across the old road.'

Godfrey Dhu saw them and set his horse up the turf bank.

'The pipe fell out of me mouth and got broke,' he announced.

'There's only a dottle in the bottom of mine,' Denis Freel said, 'for Sally forgot to get tobacco the fair day with all the excitement, and that pipe of Phil's would take a horse to draw it.'

'He's never done trying to steal it from me,' Phil said, stretching his pipe to Godfrey Dhu.

'The Knife's none the worse I hope,' Denis Freel said.

'He's all sore, but he'll be good as new in a week, the Doctor says; and if Doctor Henry is not looking after him, go again to it.'

'They say it was a terrible fight; Sam Rowan is supposed to have said in the forge that there's not a man in the Lagan would stand up to The Knife if he had room to work himself.'

'The Knife says Sam would be more than a match for him,' Godfrey Dhu said.

'Your Brian, I wish him rest, had the same habit,' Phil Burns commented. 'I never heard him say yet he could beat a man, and he was the boy could beat them.'

'I would be afraid that things will get worse,'

Denis Freel said. 'I was just sayin' to Phil that there's the Lagan out in the fields below there in the sun, and there's no tellin' how much anger is growing among the crops.'

'Well I was just batin' the whole Lagan myself,' Godfrey Dhu confessed.

'Our fightin' day is over,' Phil Burns said. 'Not but if it comes but I'd be into it. I had the best shot of the three of ye, when we were after the geese long ago.'

'Me own right eye went back on me early,' Godfrey Dhu said.

'I never like guns,' Denis Freel confessed. 'I used to have a great shot with a sling: I saw me taking down a hawk. If I spotted Carson maybe I'd be better than either of you.'

'Let Carson and Dan Sweeney fight it out,' Godfrey Dhu said. 'Dan's a great man to the young fellows.'

'We know Dan,' Phil Burns said. 'I wouldn't like any neighbour boys to come much under Dan's influence.'

'The way it is, ould men can only look on these times; they can only look on.'

'I'm going over to Big William for a pup he promised me,' Godfrey Dhu said. 'Maybe we'd go in sometime, the three of us, and say a mouthful to Dan Sweeney,' he added, back over his shoulder.

'Godfrey Dhu would be havin' meaning in that,' Denis Freel said.

'There's manliness in Godfrey Dhu,' Phil Burns said, struggling to his feet to get back to his work.

CHAPTER FOURTEEN

THE fair night was settling down into the sediment of drained days. Already planter and native were exchanging wry smiles. There had been no prosecution of The Knife, and there was no competition for honours between him and Sam Rowan. The harvest crowded in on the busy workers in the fields, and in the gaps between the showers men sweated into forgetfulness of an evening's madness. Doctor Henry in his leisurely calls on planter and native alike noted the fall in the bitterness, and went on his way rejoicing. Talk was of the harvest, of births and deaths, of sickness, and of the wisps of scandal that blew across the Lagan as the days passed.

'The patient's doing fine,' the Doctor said one evening when on his way home he noticed two trial teams in a football match. 'It's the sort of mixture I would prescribe myself,' he enthused.

And the bang of the football drew adventurous children from their tasks and sent them racing across the empty harvest fields of the Lagan.

That night came down with gusts of wind that were smoothed by a shower, and then stars peeped into the sky, and the windows of the Lagan blinked through the shadows: mild, timid stars below the feelingless glitter of the heavens. A youth toiled out his few notes on a flute, a drunk man drawled his crying 'come all ye' as his patient horse guided the way home. The Lagan was at rest.

The Rowans, in the house that had seen generations of Rowans, slow of word and of act, were collected round their fire of black turf, old man Rowan leaning forward on his stick to spit easily into the heart of the blaze.

The Montgomery kitchen was full of sound and merry talk, where long ago the dull accents of the Montgomerys had been softened by the sough of the trees that stirred to the life in themselves.

Skulking among the trees outside, Billy White hovered along the edge of the garden. He had crawled up to the very edge of the mearn, and now flitted along the fringe as perhaps one of the native stock in other days had spied upon the new-comers; Billy among his stock was restless.

And then the Fates stirred the dice and hurried the pace of the play.

'I think I'll slip down to the town an' see Weldon,' Sam Rowan said, getting up to get his bicycle.

'It's a fine, starry night. Light my bicycle lamp, Breslin, an' I'll go for a short spin,' Nuala said.

Nuala banged into Sam Rowan as she came out the gate. She fell violently on the road, and one hand was cut by the gravel. Sam picked up the bicycle; Nuala had been promptly on her feet. When she reached for the handle-bars Sam saw the blood, but she laughed, and made light of it. In his saddle-bag was a first-aid outfit; he got it out, smiling ever so slightly at a passing thought.

'Let me fix yer hand,' he said. 'I'm rough, maybe, but I'm effective.'

Inside the gate the stream ran pleasantly over grey pebbles. He washed her hand, and uncorked the iodine.

'You'll feel this a bit,' he said.

Billy White had drawn near, moving like a setter, and halting with one foot raised, he saw Rowan holding Nuala's hand. He did not catch the words, but sensitive to the tone of Sam's voice he detected the feeling in it. With difficulty he suppressed a scream. Suddenly he turned round and burst into the trees. Neither of the two at the stream had seen him.

Nuala and Sam continued sitting for a few minutes after the hand had been tied up; her face was in the shade, and her eyes were on Sam Rowan.

'I'm all right now,' she said abruptly, getting to her feet. 'Really it was nothing.'

But she limped when she got up.

'Yer knee is cut, maybe,' he said. 'Look here, go in home and see. Take this iodine. Take these things. They're a peace-offering.'

Her face was in the light of the bicycle lamp now. She took the peace-offering. Her right knee was paining her; she nodded to him, and turned home. Sam pushed the bicycle down the avenue for a few yards, and left her. Paddy Breslin got a peep at Sam on his way back to the gate, for Breslin had taken to scouting round after Billy White, and he made grimaces in the dark.

Billy had continued his headlong rush across the fields. Instinctively he ran home. The heavy waddle that marked his walking was now replaced by an awkward jog. He threw out one leg like a milch cow running, his jaws champed. Now and then he opened them to let out his thin, sudden cry. A rabbit might have made it under terror of a weasel.

He came panting into the kitchen. His aunt was out. A black fire resisted the tongues of flame that licked up stray pipes of gas and struggled to ignite the new turf. He sat down on a chair and again the sudden pained cry escaped him. He put one arm across his head with his eyes buried in the hollow of the elbow. A child might have sought to shut out a terrifying sight that way. He stamped his feet on the flags, and flung his two arms, stiff as pokers, straight in front of him. His right hand swept round in an arch and felt for the bowl of milk that rested beside the plate of porridge on the table. He put his thumb on the spoon, and gulped down the milk. With his head thrown back he drank, his eyes peering over the rim of the bowl.

His eyes, wide and uncertain as a cow's, suddenly lit up, and then narrowed and blazed. They were resting on the shot-gun on the brace. He ceased to drink, stopping so suddenly that milk flowed down his chin. He got to his feet, his eyes still on the gun. His dark face lighted, and one long, dark tooth showed where his upper lip curled slightly. He reached up and took down the gun. He fondled it. Then his eye went sharply to the window. He went over and tucked in the corner of the window blind, crossed to the dresser, and pushed plates aside to get at the cartridges. He selected a No. 2 cartridge, slipped it into the breach, and put others in his pocket. Then he turned down the light, listened inside the door for a few minutes, and stole softly into the night.

He headed straight for Montgomerys. He ran, again with that heavy, swinging jog, but he made no noise as his feet went lightly over twigs. He pushed through a gap in the hedge and took his stand under a tree. To his ears came the well-known farmyard sounds. He detected the breathing of an overfed cow, the snoring of pigs, a horse's hoof on the cobble-stones; sleeping hens murmuring in their dreams. Billy's eyes were on the kitchen door; he had not yet defined his intentions. He had moved under the impulse of madness that had descended on him when he had seen Sam Rowan and Nuala Godfrey Dhu together. Sam's defence of the Godfrey Dhus flashed with terrible meaning across Billy's mind. His senses reeled until his mind was swept of all thought before the flood of hate, long repressed, that now seethed and burned a-tremble for expression. In one wild pæan his madness called for the blind, sudden destruction of the Godfrey Dhus.

Under the tree Billy looked inside his mind for directions; he would kill Hugh Godfrey Dhu. Hugh was the one who would get the farm. Hugh was the one who would take root; stocky, box-shouldered Hugh. He spat out. His eyes were on the kitchen door, his ears, alert as a wild animal's, almost moved. And he was patient now, and cool.

He thought of The Knife, and he glanced sharply round. The idea of shooting The Knife came up. He became suddenly aware of the moon rising over the gable and crouched closer to the bark of a tree.

The idea of shooting The Knife flitted past. He would shoot Hugh, stocky, box-shouldered Hugh, or the little bitch, Nuala. Aye, he would shoot her; the restless bitch, he would shoot the eyes out of her. Rage tore him; he would shoot her. In his rage his thought leaped across the break in his courage to the idea of shooting The Knife. As his rage mounted, that idea raced freely. The Knife. He didn't fear The Knife; if he could only get The Knife faced in the doorway. A burst of laughter floated out the open kitchen door. He raised his gun instinctively, and pointed at the lighted window. He lowered it; a calf walked across the yard, and he raised his gun again; any live thing of the Godfrey Dhus.

And then suddenly he stiffened alert, this time cold, attentive. He had forgotten his anger, his actions were instinctive. A light appeared in a window upstairs. The window was blindless; a man's figure, stocky, box-shouldered Hugh. The gun swept upwards. The man and gun were immovable for a second, while one of the keenest eyes in the Lagan gazed down the sights. The foresight was uncertain, he jerked the muzzle upward, and lowered it cautiously. He could see now, and there under the sight was a living thing of the Godfrey Dhu household. He pressed the trigger. A flash. A crash. He saw Hugh fall. Without a sound he backed away in among the trees, and went home, walking with his heavy waddle and humming softly to himself to no tune he had ever heard.

The report of the gun silenced the kitchen. The Knife got to his feet; the tinkle of falling glass on the street. He swept the window curtain aside. Nuala was the first up the stairs. The Knife was at her heels. Hugh was struggling to his feet, blood gushing from his neck.

'I'm shot,' he said quietly.

The Knife pushed back the table, and stretched him full on the floor.

'Leave him to me, Knife,' Curran, the ex-soldier, said. 'Ride like the devil for a doctor.'

The Knife rushed out of the room and, vaulting the stairs, ran to the stable. He took out the mare, flung a bridle on her, and leaping on her bare back, tore wildly up the road. The Doctor was in bed after a long night case, when he pulled up at his house, but he knew the Doctor's window, and standing on the horse's back, tapped it with his finger, calling. The Doctor came across the room, and stared at the face at the window.

'Who the blazes?' he demanded, perplexed.

'Doctor Henry,' The Knife said quietly, 'will you please hurry? Hugh has been shot.'

'That you, Knife?'

'It is. Won't you hurry, please?'

'I'll hurry. Throw open the garage for me. I'll race.'

After throwing open the garage, The Knife rode to the curate's. It was James who answered his knock.

'Will ye ask Father Burns to hurry to our place?'

Burns became excited. The atmosphere of guns had yet a definite effect on him. And shooting . . . He shivered freely. 'Dead is he?' he asked in a whisper.

'That's what I don't know.'

'Is it a raid for the rifles? Yer sure nobody would give away any names if the guns are caught.'

'For heaven's sake tell Father Burns to hurry,' The Knife exploded.

James disappeared in the door, his own excitement now driving him to tell the news. The Knife rode home.

CHAPTER FIFTEEN

THE KNIFE's mind now searched for an explanation of this deed. It was an act arising directly out of Orange hostility, but whose was the hand? Billy White's face jumped into his mind. And it was as though he searched the living Billy with his eyes. His mistake was that he examined Billy with reference to the possibility of shooting himself. He could not feel that Billy would dare any such thing, not alone anyway. He put Billy aside; he did not quite dismiss him. He thought of others in the district. Then it suddenly occurred to him that the assassin had been brought in for the purpose. That thought gripped. And who would be responsible locally? But any Orangeman would feel the desire to drive them out of Montgomerys. Flaming anger swept through him, and unconsciously he urged the horse onward.

Suddenly he distinguished figures moving across the field to the front, seeking to intercept him. The party that had done the shooting? He slackened his pace. He could easily jump the mare over the hedge and make his way home across the fields, but he delayed: let them come. Then he recognised Breslin's shape; he pulled up. Breslin, Curran and three others were there. They had two shot-guns and were masked.

''Twas Sam Rowan shot Hugh,' Curran said. 'Breslin saw him.'

The Knife turned to Breslin. He didn't speak.

'I saw him inside the gate,' Breslin said, 'about half an hour before the shooting.'

The theory of the strangers led by locals returned to The Knife.

'There's only one thing for it. Hit back as hard as ye get. Hit at once. We'll get Sam Rowan should we roost him in the house.'

Rowan's home was only a few hundred yards distant. Light streamed down the avenue from the open door. The Knife slid off the horse's back.

'Take the horse home you,' he said to one of the five.

'You go home, Knife. Be you able to account for yourself. Ye'll be the one they'd jump. You go and we'll wait. You be with the doctor at the time, we'll wait.'

'How is Hugh?' The Knife asked.

'Doctor said there's a chance, just a chance.'

The Knife's face set. 'Take the horse home,' he said, and started off towards Rowan's house.

Without knocking The Knife tramped in on the floor. Sam was at the head of the table reading *The Belfast Telegraph*. The father was sitting in his chair, leaning forward and coughing.

Curran and Gallagher had shot-guns. The sight of them brought the old man Rowan to his feet.

'What's this?' he wheezed. 'What's this?' he demanded, tapping the floor with his stick. 'What's the meaning of this?' he added, hobbling across the hearth to take his place beside his son. Sam had got to his feet too. He spoke no word. His eyes were on The Knife, he didn't seem to notice the others.

The Knife strode up until he was less than an arm's length from Sam. 'Sam Rowan,' he said in a low, tense voice, 'did you do this thing?'

'What thing, Knife?' Sam asked, after a pause. The accident to Nuala had crossed his mind in the interval, but he dismissed it, the first time since it happened that evening that he had driven it completely from his mind. The Knife's gaze was biting into Sam's eyes.

'Ye don't know what I mean, Sam.'

'I don't know what ye mean, Knife.'

The barrel of Curran's rifle passed alongside The Knife and pointed at Sam's head. Sam gave it a glance, but his gaze returned to The Knife. The Knife put his hand to the barrel of the rifle and pushed it up. He looked away from Sam.

'Hugh has been shot,' he said simply.

Sam Rowan took a step forward. He put a hand on The Knife's shoulder and swung him round. 'Knife, do you believe I had hand, act or part in that thing?'

'I don't, Sam.' The Knife turned his back to the Rowans and motioned the crowd out.

'What were ye doin' in the avenue?' Breslin demanded.

There was an interruption. Doctor Henry and Nuala appeared in the doorway. The youth who had brought the horse home had told his story to Nuala.

'Surely to God, Sam, you had no act or part in this?'

'He had no act or part in it, Nuala,' The Knife said.

Nuala staggered against The Knife and he put his arm round her.

'What was he doin' in the avenue?' Breslin persisted.

'There was nothing in that,' Nuala whispered to her brother.

'Get out now,' The Knife said.

Nuala and he moved to the door. Sam Rowan came up behind them.

'I'm terribly sorry about this,' he said.

Nuala turned her head and looked at him for a second. Then she nodded seriously. The Doctor drove Nuala and The Knife home.

'He was value for a shot,' Breslin grunted outside. 'If I had had one of the guns . . .' but nobody heeded him.

CHAPTER SIXTEEN

Mary Burns hurried out with the news to her mother, and Dan Sweeney overtaking her in the village drove her out. Molly Burns had been going about the house in a pair of Phil's boots, and she had barely time to change them and get on a clean apron after the car appeared before she heard the dog bark. She gave a sweep round to the hearth and then went outside with a dish of hens' meat as an excuse. Mary was showing Dan the view, making a delay and giving the dog good time to bark a warning to the folk inside.

'I suppose the news of last night didn't reach you yet?' Dan Sweeney said, shaking hands.

Molly showed her fright.

'No, no, all your folk are well,' he hastened to assure her.

Molly moistened her lips with her tongue. 'With the way the papers are full of talk a person bes nervous. . . .'

'One of the Godfrey Dhus was shot last night,' Mary said.

'What kind of a family are they?' Molly said. 'They're always in trouble; there's always something.'

Dan Sweeney nodded. 'They won't be said by anybody,' he said, making a gesture of hopelessness.

'Father Burns did his best for them, but they know more than the priest.'

'God help them,' Mary prayed. 'There's some darkness over them.'

Dan Sweeney would not delay; he just called because he didn't like to be so close and not darken the light in the door. He shook hands again and hurried off. Molly was in a hurry for him to go so that she might hear the news. She bolted the door when she and Mary were back in the kitchen after Dan Sweeney had driven off.

'This one beyond will be sendin' one of the children in to see what they can pick up,' she explained. 'Now we can talk in peace.'

Mary was full of news. The whole Lagan had poured in on Montgomerys, and everybody was for doing everything until Dan Sweeney sent James down to take charge of the grounds. People that were there had told Mary that James was like a general drilling men among the trees, and being saluted, and behaving like a duke. All the men were lined up and told that they were the Lagan Battalion, and Father John blessed them.

'Will James get into any trouble, do you think?' Molly asked.

'I heard Dan Sweeney argue that with Father John. He said that it would take careful leadership to keep people quiet and that's why he made James rush in and take charge. He said the Inspector of Police would be glad of it; only keep that quiet because the heart was in people's mouths the way James edged the police out of everything. The old master said the like of it wasn't since Brian Boru.'

'James will be a member of parliament yet, praises be to God. I knew there was something good keepin' James from passin' his examinations,' Molly enthused.

'An' everybody is talkin' about himself and Nuala Godfrey Dhu. She's daft about him: it's always volunteers, volunteers, with her. Just an excuse that anybody could see through. I could take a pick at her this minute, she's that important and sure of herself.'

'James has his weakness and a good, strong woman might be a back to him. And there's no knowing what money they have; and she's the only girl.'

'But she's always talkin' war, war, and killin'.'

'Showin' off, you may be sure, makin' people think more and more of James; she's young, not twenty yet I hear.'

'Sometimes I think she means it.'

Then Father John will have to have a word with her,' Molly said.

'Father John and Dan Sweeney were together for hours and hours,' Mary said. 'They were in Father John's bedroom.'

'I suppose you didn't hear a word. . . .

'God forgive you, mother, I'd as soon try to listen at the confessional.'

'Will he tell you later?'

'No; but he'll be tellin' it to the banker, and he's a bit deaf. Father John and the banker is as friendly as me father and Denis Freel.'

'Indeed your father will keep with the Denis Freels. Off the two of them went to Montgomerys, and nothin' I could say would stop them.'

'He says Father John is now as watchful as you like,' Mary pleaded.

'It's Father John with them all,' Molly grumbled. 'Everybody else is Father Dunlevy, Father Coll, Father O'Gara or the like, but we made ours Father John. I can stand anybody but Sally Freel. "Are you hearing from the ones beyont?" she says yesterday morning. Ye'd think it was an ordinary man she was askin' after; I could brain her with the dish cloth.'

'She was always trahan; just burning with jealousy. She'll have a pain in the belly wondering what Dan Sweeney was doing here.'

'That she may,' Molly Burns prayed, unbolting the door. And she stood in the doorway and watched Sally Freel approach.

'I was just on the way over,' Sally said, raking back a wavelet of hair under her neck shawl, 'when Dan Sweeney's car came, and I ducked back. Next to yourself I had me bag apron on me for I was spreading dung. Denis says the crowds of the world are at Montgomerys; that not since the arrest of Father McFadden was the county so dancin' on its toes.'

'Indeed it's anxious times for them's leading the country.'

'The Godfrey Dhus must be great people out an' out when it's them the Orangemen shoot; the whole Lagan is only discoverin' that now; everybody thought indeed it wasn't them was the leaders.' Sally held up her knitting between her and the light to count the stitches on a needle.

'It's hard to change ignorant people's talk.'

'The rumour's goin' round now that Godfrey

Dhu's the grandson of Manus O'Donnell that beat the dragoon at Lifford.'

'You can be sure it's some people's tongues drew trouble on the Godfrey Dhus,' Molly said, flinging a fallen coal back into the blaze.

'Hoigh, Sally,' Denis Freel called, urgently from the outside.

'Denis'll kill me, sure as death,' Sally said, putting up her knitting. 'I often say,' she continued, turning towards her neighbour, 'I often say that I pity you your worry with Father John and James up to their two eyes in the trouble; but I suppose everybody has their crosses.'

Denis was waiting for Sally.

'Damn bit better yourself and Molly are than a pair of childer; can't ye let her be? I'm sick and tired of the two of ye nippin' and nippin' at one another.'

'How do ye know what we were sayin'?' Sally challenged.

'Didn't I see you sailin' across the garden. There's two families over there that was twenty years bad friends, an' all over a dog fight; wouldn't that be a lesson to you?'

'It's true for ye, Denis; but the sight of herself and her hat every Sunday morning keeps me on edge for the week.'

'There's a weakness in her on the mother's side,' Denis urged.

'Then God help her, for it's little help I'm to her,' Sally repented, tying on her bag apron to get back to spreading the dung. 'I'll have to get a hold on my tongue,' she added, beginning her work.

CHAPTER SEVENTEEN

The Knife drove into the market with a cart of pigs. He let down the cart and took the horse across to a stable and from there he went across to the court-house to pay the rates. He was coming out of the court-house door when Billy White emerged from a laneway, and went swaggering along the foot-path. Billy did not see The Knife, who was about to go back to his cart when the police sergeant, passing Billy White, wagged a playful, admonitory finger at him, and there flashed into The Knife's mind the thought that the sergeant too had heard the rumours that floated about the Lagan as to who had shot Hugh. The Knife strolled slowly after White. A local magistrate passed, and Billy meeting his greetings swaggered more and more. He swung one arm in long awkward sweeps and banged himself on the thigh. He halted at the door of a public-house and put his two hands before young Weldon, who was coming out, and horseplayed him back into the bar. The Knife followed them in.

There were not many people in the bar, and no-body spoke to The Knife, who stood with his elbows on the counter without heeding the fussing barman. Billy had gone over to join a group of his friends at the far end of the bar and his back was towards The Knife. Young Weldon met The Knife's stare and fidgeted with a glass. Talk died down among the group; somebody tramped on Billy White. He turned round and met The Knife's gaze, moved his feet and laughed. He reached for his drink and gulped it down.

Billy's importance had been growing during the past week. Girls of his race had stopped him here and there and told him he was the only man in the Lagan. He had seen the inscription 'Fenians Beware!' on the dead walls of the Lagan, and he knew the threat was based on his act; it was more than a threat, it was a verdict. That morning for the first time the dead walls had carried a reply: 'Up the Godfrey Dhus!' had been painted on the old church wall. And now this entrance of The Knife was like a shout of that same slogan. Rage flashed in him. He hammered his glass on the counter, and when it was filled he came towards The Knife, at whose elbow now stood a pint of stout.

Billy threw back his head and laughed. 'I'll give you a toast,' he challenged.

The Knife remained relaxed against the counter.

'Up, Carson!' Billy roared, raising his glass.

With a quick, instinctive impulse, The Knife responded. 'Up, the Godfrey Dhus!'

Billy's glass halted in mid-air, his brown eyes lit up with a new anger that Billy's mind could not brake, all his self-conceit now challenged.

'Up me, be God!' Billy roared.

With a flick of his shoulder The Knife was erect.

He dashed his bottle of stout into Billy's face, and then with a quick swing he caught Billy's chin with his fist and toppled the Orangeman senseless in the corner. And then, his anger still dominating the bar, he walked out.

CHAPTER EIGHTEEN

Doctor Henry drove up to Sam Rowan's. Sam was out in the fields, and only Rebecca was in the kitchen. William was asleep, and she raised a finger for silence, so the Doctor tiptoed out. Sam saw him coming and sat down on an upturned creel.

'I'm that keyed up, Sam, I'm liable to break something. Did something out of the common happen at the meeting last night?'

'That would be a way to put it,' Sam agreed.

'Well just suppose you let me have it.'

'Billy White went mad and nearly killed the man from Belfast.'

'And what put Billy mad?'

'Breaking the covenant.'

'And the covenant's broken?'

'Aye, it's broken; we're to come under Home Rule in Donegal, Monaghan and Cavan.'

The Doctor sat down on a stump of wood.

'I touch earth,' he sighed with relief.

'It's a quare and unexpected day for the Lagan,' Sam said gravely.

The Doctor was silent.

'Is this a secret?' he asked, after a pause.

'There was a bit of hubbub at the close, but there's not likely anybody'll be anxious to say it.'

'And Home Rule is coming,' the Doctor mused. 'Why aren't they told? It would ease down the soldiering and play-acting; we may as well begin to be neighbours with our neighbours.'

'It'll be hard on some of the ould people,' Sam said, picking at a rod with a finger-nail.

'What happened Billy White?'

'He just lost his senses,' Sam said. 'It took half of us to hold him.'

'And what was the reason for the decision to break the covenant?' Doctor Henry asked.

'It seems it was nae a covenant but some politician's trick that didn't come off. The Orangemen of the rest of Ulster are going to let go of their promises to us. They'll escape Home Rule round Belfast.'

'Are you afraid to come under Home Rule, Sam?'

'It'll about kill them inside,' Sam said, nodding towards his home.

'I'd like to tell The Knife, Sam; is there anything agin telling?'

'If the other crowd get screechin' about it,' Sam said, doubtfully.

'He won't,' Doctor Henry said. 'Well, I'm damned, Sam, but if anybody had said that to the Orangemen of the Lagan when Carson was here . . . There's one other thing, Sam, that worries me; that's about Billy. The Knife knows.'

Sam ceased toying with the rod. 'That's bad,' he said. 'That's bad.'

'He'll be sure to do something about it, Sam.'

'And there's a big backing for Billy; now when everything should be quieting, it's bad.'

Carabine barked angrily.

'Talk of the devil,' Doctor Henry said.

The Knife came striding across to them. 'I was in town looking for you,' he said to Doctor Henry. 'Will you go over and see Billy White?'

Doctor Henry groaned and stooped wearily for his hat.

'Breslin and Curran are with him, but he has the strength of ten.'

'Breslin and Curran are with him?' the Doctor said, puzzled.

The Knife nodded. 'I went over to him this morning as soon as I saw him afoot; what for doesn't matter now. It was while I was wrestling with him to take the gun from him I noticed something wrong; he had the ould woman locked in the room, and she near dead with fright. I set her free, and sent her for Breslin, and we tied him up. He's mad.'

'Knife, I take off my hat to you,' the Doctor said quietly. 'I'm able to breathe again. Tell him, Sam.'

'They broke the covenant, Knife,' Sam said, after a pause, 'and we're to come in under Home Rule; they made a bargain for themselves in Belfast.'

'An' you're not goin' to fight agin' it in the Lagan, Sam?'

'We're fightin' no more in the Lagan,' Sam said.

'Well, it's no wonder poor Billy White went as he did,' The Knife said. 'Well, you'll be welcome under Home Rule, Sam.'

'It's a bit hard on the ould folk,' Sam said. 'There's long roots to what they think.'

That Home Rule could mean quiet pain like this

had not occurred to The Knife: anger, yes, but pain . . .

'Well, ye can keep it from them till it comes, anyway,' he said, turning away.

And now with Home Rule on the doorstep, Middle Class Ireland queued up for the offices that were to be given out. There was just a little confusion in the queue, and awkward entanglements from conflicting promises by those up near the treasure chest. The confusion in the queue might have developed were it not that a note of alarm rang out sharply and smothered the squabble. New men appeared suddenly and called on the people to push forward in arms for separation from the British Empire. The queue roared out lustily against any such teaching, mocking the new teachers, and warning the masses of the frightful results of following them. Pearse, Clarke, Connolly, MacDermott, and the others were bad men; they were likely to spoil the case for Home Rule which rested so much on a guarantee of loyalty to the British crown, so they were traitors. They were endangering the offices of the friends of the great host of clergymen, so they were anti-religious. Pious people would spurn them, zealous ones attack them; it was a great day for Ireland when they were nearly murdered in Limerick. Ireland was loyal to the Empire; Home Rule depended on loyalty.

And then one day a couple of hundred Dublin workmen, a couple of score of students, a handful of intellectuals, came out into the streets of Dublin, and proclaimed an Irish Republic. Never did a queue roar as the Home Rule queue roared then; they screeched loyalty, they turned out to assist the British to restore order, and called loudly for the blood of the leaders. Priests, who had been holding places in the queues for less presentable relatives, leapt into the pulpit and hurled curses at the workmen of Dublin.

And the Orangemen laughed. Home Rule was back fifty years, they told one another, and received the apologies of loyal natives with sympathetic attention, and encouraged them to go on with their declaration of loyalty to the Empire, and destruction of the insurgents.

But, outside the queue, a picture persisted, and sounds recurred; the picture of the men of Dublin, bare-breasted amid a hurricane of steel, the protecting city ripped from around them, and the ring of death closing in; and the sounds, the crackle of rifles at the dawn. . . .

And soon the gods will play their grim joke, and the workers of Ireland will leap into the fight that had caught them unprepared, or nervous; they will turn angrily on the queue and pelt it into obscurity; the quicklime graves will release a rush of feeling and set ablaze a fight for freedom that will blot out the scramble for office. And with the passing days, the 'wise men' of Ireland will recognise in the heroism of the Irish masses the technique for the restoration of the case for Home Rule. The garrison gang, thriving on the abortive rebellion, must now be met with such a storm of hostility to British rule that the Government in London may learn that Ireland cannot, without serious embarrassment, be held within the Empire except through the creation of a new garrison cast.

The wise men whisper, and are convinced, and they enter the struggle calling loudly to the men of Ireland to press forward. Pearse and Clarke are rescued from hell, and handed over to the excited nation as saints. Connolly is a human being again, his death having condoned his socialism, not enthroned it. The voices of the old garrison will soon be drowned, and while the fighting men of Ireland struggle and die, the queueing will be renewed. But meantime, down in the Lagan . . .

CHAPTER NINETEEN

Doctor Henry and Sam Rowan came across the river and took the path up to Montgomerys. The Knife saw them coming, and was puzzled. Nuala saw them through the kitchen window, and paused in her work. The Doctor's calling would not have puzzled her much, for he came in, off and on, since Hugh's trouble; but Sam Rowan had never been there, and now here were both. Curran and Breslin and James Burns were in the kitchen, and they crowded to the window to watch the two men approach. The Knife joined them, and then moved with them towards the open kitchen door.

'The trouble must be spreading, and they're coming to look for shelter,' Breslin suggested.

Nuala shook her head, and was silent.

The Doctor entered the kitchen first. He nodded to everybody. Nuala held out her hand; she shook hands with Sam Rowan too.

'It's a bad sign of neighbours when a body shakes hands with them,' she said.

'It's not too bad when she does,' Sam said.

'I never thought you were that ready in the tongue, Sam Rowan,' she said.

'I'm ready enough in things that have meanin' to me,' he said.

'The fight is over in Dublin, and they're killin' the leaders now,' Doctor Henry said, tearing a corner off an envelope to make a light for his pipe.

'They're sure to murder all round them when they win,' Nuala said quickly.

'It's a bad business,' Sam Rowan said, 'a bad business.'

'The bad business is that we let the men in Dublin be murdered without a blow,' The Knife said.

'Well, it's over now, and what you intended doin' and had no chance to do is a thing that nothing is gained by sayin' now,' Sam Rowan said.

'I suppose there was some meanin' in the two of you comin'?' The Knife said.

'There was,' the Doctor said, 'a meaning in it.'

'And what would the meaning be.'

'The police and the soldiers will be coming,' Doctor Henry said.

'So they're coming,' The Knife said.

There was no word spoken in the kitchen for a minute.

'That was thoughtful of you two,' Nuala said.

'Suppose we draw up chairs and begin to have a chat,' the Doctor said, and as he spoke lorries came into view in the brae.

'I wouldn't attempt to run out the back,' Sam Rowan said sharply to Burns, 'they'd maybe fire.'

'I'm not right clear about lettin' you two shield us,' The Knife said.

'I'm all for neighbourliness, Knife, and we're neighbours, and it would be quare now if you were less in your own house.'

A motor throbbed up the drive; there was a tramp of feet in the street.

The police inspector was about to give an order when he recognised Sam Rowan sitting facing the door. Sam nodded a greeting. The officer entered, puzzled.

'I didn't expect to find a party like this here.'

'Had you any business with us?' The Knife asked.

'Could I have a word with you, Rowan?'

'You could if you speak from where you are.'

'Are you able to answer for these people's loyalty?'

'I'm not able to answer for myself sometimes,' Sam said seriously.

'That's strange talk,' the officer said.

'My bad influence, Mr. Knight,' the Doctor interposed. 'I spent two years colouring water, licking labels, and deluging the inside of your countrymen with medicine, and I'm against the Empire since; panel experience in London made an Irishman of me.'

'These are no days for such talk, Doctor Henry.'

'Arrest me, and I'll repeat them in my speech from the dock; I'll proclaim my convictions from the scaffold; I love no nation that's so thirsty after medicine.'

'Search the house,' the officer ordered. 'Which of you is The Knife?' he asked, after a sergeant had reported back.

'I am,' The Knife said, without changing his position where he leaned against the open door.

'I may have to arrest you.'

The Knife made no reply; nobody spoke.

'It would help me on my way to ripe treason,' Doctor Henry said.

'I may say I didn't expect you two here,' the officer said.

'And I'm very sure I'll quit calling if you keep coming,' the Doctor answered. 'Is that Major White I see,' he continued, getting to his feet. "'Pon my soul it is; Major, I'm being arrested.'

'You should be hanged; that damn motor bike you loaned me is cross-eyed and spavined.'

Sam Rowan came out on the street too. The officer pulled at his moustache and stood irresolute.

'Could you give me a lift back to town, Mr. Knight?' the Doctor said, turning to include him in the talk with the major.

'I may tell you your presence here embarrasses me greatly,' the officer grumbled, moving slowly away.

'Ireland is an embarrassing country,' the Doctor said. 'I tell you, Mr. Knight, the way Englishmen guzzle bottles of medicine simply turns me against your countrymen.'

'Oh, go to hell!' the police officer said, striding off.

'Nuala, you'll have to teach me a Fenian song,' Doctor Henry said. 'What was yon one, Sam?'

Sam growled, and strolled off without saying a word to anybody, and the Doctor chuckled as he went after him.

CHAPTER TWENTY

Nora Dan Sweeney stuck out the tricolour from her window on a fair day, and a crowd gathered under it, cheering. Dan Sweeney himself had been away at an auction, and he arrived when the excitement was at its height. Dan had heard no word of sympathy with the 'mad doings in Dublin,' and it was only a blood-poisoned foot that had kept him from the council meeting where their treachery had been denounced. Father Burns had come out good and strong against the enemies of Home Rule, everybody in fact, except the Godfrey Dhus and the few servant men under their influence. Dan's first thought on seeing the flag was of his post office, and his impulse was to drive in angrily into the mob; but the crowd was cheering, and the bar was packed. He turned sharply out a bye-road; he had meadows out there anyway. When he came back the fair was still crowded round his door, and the flag was gone. A group of police came out of his house and pushed their way through the crowd. Right in the centre of the throng, Dan Sweeney and the D.I. came face to face.

'I regret your absence made our interference necessary,' the officer said.

'What was wrong?' Dan demanded.

'This flag was flying from one of your windows.'

'And what's wrong with the flag?'

'It's not the flag of a loyal subject.'

'And who said I was a loyal subject?' Dan challenged.

Those within hearing yelled, and the police struggled out through a hostile crowd, and word went out across the Lagan that evening that Dan Sweeney was a mad Sinn Feiner.

The enthusiasm of the fair set the young men parading the town and cheering. From archways insults were hurled at the police and a drunk man was torn from a group of constables. Police whistles screamed, and the crowd booed, disappearing into open doors, and into yards to meet again in groups at cross-roads, and there the talk turned on re-building the volunteers that had gone out of conceit with themselves, following their failure to be called into conflict in 1916.

Dan Sweeney presided at the meeting, and James Burns again took command. And after the meeting James Burns hurried to Montgomerys, where out among the trees he talked to Nuala of the day that would come soon when the men of the Lagan would play their part for certain.

CHAPTER TWENTY-ONE

Doctor Henry came on Phil Burns and Denis Freel where they sheltered from a shower under a hedge, Phil's waterproof across both heads. The rain pelted on the hedge behind them, and pattered on the coat. The Doctor was wearing a suit of oilskins, and was on his way to the lake.

'A shower's a grand thing when you have a shelter,' the Doctor greeted, crushing in under the top branches of the hedge. 'I always like the patter of the rain when it can't get at me.'

'I get no good of it,' Phil Burns said, 'barrin' I can smoke; every drop makes me teeth water else.'

'Will you try a fill out of this stuff?' the Doctor offered, reaching out his pouch to Denis Freel.

'Soul will I,' Denis said, feeling in his waistcoat pocket for a knife to empty out his pipe. 'Phil here wouldn't take a thing save black twist for a pension.'

'I'm that way,' Phil agreed. 'Things I'm used to is what I like. Molly got a new brand of tea there, and I used to be ashamed of myself sneakin' over to Sally Freel for a sup; it was dearer tea, but I had no taste for it. Am the same with dickeys; there's people be's like that; they can't change.'

'It's a bad time for them that can't change, inside

anyway,' the Doctor said. 'What do two sensible men like you think about the way the country is going?'

'It's mixed,' Denis Freel said. 'Like most troubles in Ireland there'll be a bad end, am afraid.'

'I was sorry about the rising,' Doctor Henry said. 'They were grand men that were killed, but Home Rule would have been here only for them: now them that were for Home Rule have gone on further.'

'People wants more than Home Rule now,' Phil Burns said.

'And would the two of you now want more?'

'I'm all for the whole thing,' Phil Burns said. 'Me and Denis here and Godfrey Dhu were always of that mind: am a bad hand at changin'.'

'Orangemen would be very frightened of the clear cut,' Doctor Henry said. 'It took a lot to make them give in to Home Rule, but they'd be nervous to go any further.'

'Orangemen find it hard to change,' Phil Burns agreed.

'It all seems a bit hopeless,' the Doctor said, and for a time the three men smoked in silence.

'I was noticing a man about Billy White's,' Denis Freel said. 'Is it Billy that's back?'

'Billy's back,' Doctor Henry said. 'His aunt got her brother-in-law to claim him. He's a rougher Billy than ever now. And that's another worry to me.'

'He's a lumpy nature of a man,' Phil Burns said. 'The whole breed of him was that way. I saw his father rip a dog with a hook because he was beatin' a big bully of a dog he had.'

'Throth did ye, Phil,' Denis Freel encouraged.

'That was the day Brian Godfrey Dhu showed the man he was: there's men like Billy, and they're naturally thick and mean, and when they're roused they're fealltac, dangerous.'

'Breslin and Billy are a bit the same kind, and they keep darin' each other,' Denis Freel said. 'Though Breslin would never go past the flake of a stick,' he continued.

The mail car drove past down below, their eyes were on it because it was the only thing moving in the rain. Suddenly men darted into view, and the horse pulled up sharply, and rose on his haunches. The mails were handed over to masked men. Neither of the three men spoke until the raiders had cleared away, and then Doctor Henry got to his feet.

'Life is being screwed up clear of the fields,' he said, 'and soon it will have no time for the crops and the cattle and the men and women at all: it was nicer the other way, and maybe when the people come back to the old life again, they'll be that changed it won't be as nice a world to live in.'

'Hasn't he the flow of talk for an Orangeman?' Denis Freel said when he was gone.

'I'll bet you Dan Sweeney won't like raidin' the mails,' Phil Burns said. 'That he mayn't. I'd be a glad man if himself and James fell out.'

'And Godfrey Dhu will be a proud man too. The shower's over, and devil all a body does these times only runnin' in and out for news: it's true enough for the Doctor. I couldn't tell you when that black cow of mine is comin' if I was asked now.'

''Tis then, you went to the bull with her the day Sergeant Fallon had the gun and uniform taken off him down there at the bridge: and Molly has the cuttin' from the paper at home and the date.'

'They're better men than we were,' Denis Freel decided.

'The Knife is Brian Godfrey Dhu over again,' Phil Burns said. 'And he was the man. Yon's Molly callin',' he added without enthusiasm, and turned across the near way home.

CHAPTER TWENTY-TWO

It was night-time; dawn was yet some hours distant. A bright moon crept slowly across a clear sky; a few fleecy clouds hung over the hills to the north-west.

In Montgomerys all was at peace. The family was asleep, The Knife and Hugh in one room, Nuala on the same landing, the father downstairs.

The Knife awoke, a sudden full awakening, and bounded lightly out on the floor. Some instinct warned him that danger was closing in on him. He slipped into a topcoat, tripped down the stairs in the bare feet, halting in the kitchen to put his feet in his boots; he gave heed to his father's regular breathing. He darted out of the house.

A dull sound broke on his ear, some movement away back among the trees. Taking advantage of a low wall he hurried over to take shelter under a bunch of briars. Once there he remembered his gun was dumped in the bank, a few yards further away from the house. A cloud darkened the moon. He moved cautiously in the shade and reached his dump. He did not touch the gun; he just waited beside it.

He had not wakened Hugh. He thought of him now, but he had no fear for him, except the nervousness for any live thing within such dark movements. Then his thoughts were switched back to the happenings around him. Men were coming through the trees, men appeared at the back of the house, a cordon was closed round it, and a sentry took his stand within a few yards of where The Knife crouched.

He was rather fortunate in his position; he was outside the cordon though dangerously close to it. His best plan was to remain still. Any movement might have him detected and right behind him were a few yards of bare ground.

A member of the raiding party knocked on the door, knocked loudly, authoritatively. He heard the dog bark, he saw a light shine in the kitchen window. He heard the door being opened. He waited there, tempted to steal away while the party was interested in the house, yet strangely impelled to stay. Other lights appeared in the house. He wished he could have spoken to Nuala. Was Hughie safe for certain? Everybody knew Hughie wasn't strong. A figure came over towards the sentry, and with a sudden burst of something akin to fear, The Knife recognised Billy White, a madman loose with a gun. The sentry halted him.

'The blasted man is gone,' Billy White exploded. 'We missed him. Burn down the place.'

Hughie was taken out on to the street.

'Where's The Knife?' the officer who had remained outside demanded.

'Where you won't get him,' Hugh answered.

'You'll do deputy for him,' a voice taunted.

'Lucky for you,' Hugh retorted.

Billy White had a rifle in his hand, he had probably guided the raiding party: the police were to blame for that, for they must know Billy had not recovered. A terrible fear of Billy held The Knife, fear of him as an influence against his family. The sentry moved on his beat towards the group on the street. Billy remained where he was, leaning on his rifle, contemplating the people on the street. Nuala, partly dressed, attracted his gaze, and then his eyes went searching through the dark corners round about the house. Again his instinct or sensitiveness to thoughts that had reference to himself gave The Knife the feeling that Billy would detect him lurking in the shadow. Noiselessly he felt among the moss for his gun, a Colt automatic, and unwrapped it. Very gently he manipulated it and put a round in the breech. While he was still effecting it, he saw to his relief Hugh and Nuala, tall among the Tommies, cross the light from the window and go inside too. Billy's eye also was caught by the movement, but he renewed his survey of his surroundings, and across a few feet of greyness his eyes and The Knife's met. Billy's shout, the levelling of his gun, the burst of flame from the briars and from Billy's rifle, and The Knife's bound across the few exposed yards of a hillock were only the events of a moment.

Billy fell wounded. His strong, grim face was startled with a sudden amazement that was childlike. He wiped blood from his lips with the back of his hand.

They carried him hurriedly into Godfrey Dhu's kitchen and laid him on a couch. There was a doctor in attendance.

'Take me out of this house,' Billy screamed.

'Don't let me die under this man's roof. Take me away.' They held a flask to his lips. He screamed, a sound like a wounded seal. 'I'll drink nothing under this roof. Pitch me on the road, anywhere. Don't leave me here,' he pleaded. And then he fainted.

The ambulance drew up at the door and they carried him into it, and the raiding party withdrew.

Eagerly Nuala set out to seek The Knife, and Hugh followed her. She called him gently, fearfully, hopefully. But when day came to light up the well-tilled fields of the Lagan, The Knife was on his way to the mountains 'on the run.' And that evening they heard the story of how he had roused James Burns and got him clear out into the fields, just in time, before the raiders could close in. 'The trouble' had come to the Lagan in earnest.

CHAPTER TWENTY-THREE

DOCTOR HENRY and Nuala were standing on the bank of the river when a lorry swept by; rifle bullets whizzed through the trees, the soldiers were taking chance shots in among the trees. The Doctor had just come in from the mountain where he had attended a wounded man, and was giving his instructions to Nuala.

'I'm walking on the bank of a river,' he said after a pause, 'and you are sweeping past in the flood. I can't reach you; I just run along the bank waiting for the wreckage to come ashore.'

'One can so easily forget you are an Orangeman; indeed I don't think you are,' she said, smiling at him.

'I'm a neighbour among neighbours,' he said seriously. 'I would try to be more than a neighbour by you, Nuala, but your whole vitality is so mortgaged to this fight that I don't believe you have heart or passion for anything else.'

'I have a heart, Doctor Henry; you are doing as much as half a dozen, and doing work no one else could do.'

'So, Nuala, you measure everything that way. Tell me this: will you marry Burns?'

'I never think of it, Doctor Henry.'

'But he does.'

'He is a great man these times.'

'He is; but you are the Ireland he's fighting for, and you are the reward. Don't blind yourself.'

'Oh, Doctor Henry, where's the use in talk. I'm just inside in the heart of the happenings; there is passion in me, dark passion that shakes me. I pray to see the country come forward with a roar and sweep the foreigners into the sea; that's what I dream of.'

'Poor little dreamer,' the Doctor said.

'It will come,' she said, facing him.

'My God, girl, how you blaze! I would blast mountains if you could blaze like that for me.'

'Doctor Henry, please.'

'You don't see yourself as you are, Nuala: I who can feel you, know. There's Burns; that man has built up as I never believed he could: you have blazed into him until the weakness is mostly melted out of him; what he is will never be clear until he is tested beyond the range of your influence. There's Rowan; who would ever believe that Sam Rowan would hide wounded Fenians, and like doing it; the big fellow is just a piece of earth you have made vibrant, and strange ideas are breeding in Sam.'

'Sam Rowan has been splendid too,' Nuala said.

'You are so unconscious of yourself. And then there's me: I'm just head over heels in love with you, I think, and you are out there in the stream; and the end that is coming will kill folk like you.'

'I like you least when you hint like that.'

'But woman, it is not hinting. All this turmoil, all this suffering is to prove to stupid Englishmen what they should have seen in the distance, that the old garrison – that's my people – cannot hold this country, and a new garrison must be hired. 1916 made this lesson necessary. And I know you won't heed, nor will The Knife, nor Curran, nor the lads I like, and you will be walked on. When that day comes God knows what I'll do.'

'You don't talk like this with the boys?'

'I do not: I may talk so with The Knife.'

'It's the limitation of the Orangeman in you gives your views like this; this is freedom or annihilation.'

The Doctor shook his head. 'I am so clear on what my stock are losing that I can see what Dan Sweeney and his like are gaining.'

'Ireland will be one big family of workers, living for each other, when we're free,' Nuala said.

'This fighting will stop some morning and the leaders will be offered what men of my stock had, the good offices and the tasks that my stock had to face. I remember a day when old Gregg flung fistfuls of silver at the school gate with the whole school looking on; we all knew it was wrong to touch it, and stood back manfully until a daughter of Lefty Craig's picked up a half-crown that had rolled out near her; then we all dived for the money, and I tore the sleeve out of a lad's coat.'

'And what did you do with the money, Doctor Henry?'

'My mother made me leave it back,' he said.

'That's just it; something that's behind this will keep us from scrambling.' The Doctor made a gesture of helplessness and returned to his car.

CHAPTER TWENTY-FOUR

A RAID of Rowans was threatened and William Rowan sat in the corner, leaning forward on his stick staring into the fire. Sweat glistened on his forehead, his breathing was laboured. His wasted cheeks were tinged with colour, he cleared his throat repeatedly. Rebecca was standing by the room door, her thin hands resting on her wasted hips. Out in the street was the tramp of many feet, and the clamour of voices; snatches of whistling and song broke out now and then.

At the door Sam Rowan stood talking to a British officer, who explained that he had been sent to raid the house. Sam stood cross-legged leaning against the doorpost, a quiet smile on his lips. Down on the road lorries straggled along by the fence, and the toot-toot of the Doctor's small car came impudently from amid them, as the Doctor drove hurriedly up the avenue. It was the rush of the Doctor's car that brought the smile to Sam Rowan.

'Aye, raid,' he said, slowly. 'Here's Doctor Henry,' he added, nodding towards the tooting horn.

'Yes, I left a message for him, telling him how damn sorry I was to burst in on you here; I'm sick to death of all this tossing about of beds, and pulling of homes to pieces. We can't ignore information, you'll understand, though we know much of it may be just viciousness against neighbours.'

'Most of it would be that,' Sam Rowan said.

'Major Price, this is about the far end of the limit,' Doctor Henry blurted out. 'This family is known as the Black Rowans; the whole Lagan will chuckle over this raid. But there's the old man inside, it would about kill him.'

'I am worrying about him,' Sam said thoughtfully.

'Just come inside, Major. Now listen; this family is at the root of what's loyal in the minds of the Lagan; damn it, man, if you knew the buck Fenian of Ireland was here it would be good business not to find him in it; the Lagan would just sit down and sing rebel songs for ever more if a lead was given by the Rowans; but the buck Fenian is not here,' he added.

'Will you give me your word, Mr. Rowan, that there are no rebels under your roof?'

'We're a stubborn, stiff-necked lot when we're roused,' Doctor Henry interposed, 'and this is an indignity.'

'Is it rebels under my roof?' William Rowan demanded, getting to his feet. 'Have I lived to hear an officer of the King ask that question under my roof?'

Doctor Henry rushed to the old man's side. 'It's all a mistake, William,' he said. 'It's all a mistake.' He made a face at Major Price. The perplexed officer scratched his head. 'I'll tell you what, Major,' Doctor Henry called. 'Get the men to rest themselves down there on the lawn, and we'll build a fire and cook them a feed. A demonstration of friendliness will buck up the Lagan; what the Rowans do others will follow, and it may give the local population courage to associate with you. It's a damn shame, the way even their friends tiptoe past His Majesty's forces.'

'We can't buy a damn thing in the village,' Major Price said. 'We have to go behind the counters ourselves for anything we require, and we know that the traders would be friendly if they dared. Sounds a jolly good idea of yours, Doctor, a plucky thing for you to do,' he added, turning to Sam Rowan.

'Not a bit of pluck in the world,' Sam said, 'and I'll be glad to do it.'

The few officers gathered in the garden and strolled around while the soldiers lazed about and Rebecca walked among them serving out tea and chunks of home-made bread. Old William Rowan came to the door to see the sight, and his walk was steadier than it had been for months. He waved to the cheering throng when they withdrew, and Rebecca fluttered a small Union Jack.

'I would have died with the disgrace of it, if the King's soldiers had raided my house,' William said.

'This was the happiest day I had for years and years,' Rebecca said, her eyes on the dust cloud where the lorries passed.

'I was sweatin',' Sam Rowan said to the Doctor; they were both round at the gable.

'Sweating? Man dear, I nearly swooned. We must shift them to-night.'

'We would have to do it anyway, now that

Rebecca is up and about again,' Sam said. 'And I wonder who . . . I wonder . . .'

'Would you drop over and put her mind at rest, Sam; I must race off on a sick call?'

Sam nodded and strode down towards the river, where he would meet Nuala.

CHAPTER TWENTY-FIVE

Burns wished to risk calling at Montgomerys. The Godfrey Dhu household were asleep. The east was yielding an ooze flight out through rents in black clouds, and soft whispers washed in the darkness among the trees. Burns and The Knife whispered in the avenue a little distance from the gate. They had come through the rain and the gloom of a long, featureless night tramp, returning from an inter-brigade discussion, and were on their way back to their dug-out in the hills. It was James who was urging the call; The Knife was listening to James arguing that it would be safe to run in for a few minutes and have a hurried drink of tea. As he talked, James's eye wandered to an open window where window curtains danced; Nuala's window, he knew. And The Knife knew that it was the thought of Nuala was driving James Burns to risk a delay at a place so often raided as Godfrey Dhus.

It was not that they had not ventured in there on and off; indeed, a dive home was not anything more risky than lots of calls The Knife made; but he was vaguely uneasy. He was tired too, and he would rather not delay until he could fall into a bed to sleep. He had been on his feet many more hours than

Burns, and he lacked the stimulus to break the journey that was influencing James.

'It's bad to get nervy,' James said sulkily. 'Let's go.'

The Knife jerked his cap down on his forehead and led the way. There would be a fire, with the kettle hung high up, and the teapot by the fireside, with bread and butter and milk ready on the table. 'I'll make the tea damn quick,' The Knife thought, and he grinned; he would see that the tea was made and that Burns and he struck the road again without calling Nuala. He glanced round, and the grin wore off his lips when he saw Burns gazing at the bedroom window. His mood softened; he had been snarlish with Burns; he felt a bit mean, and he turned aside among the trees.

'Fling something at the window, and Nuala will let us in,' he called across to Burns.

He heard the patter of gravel against the glass, and he chuckled to himself; Nuala would not be in the least deceived, but he hoped she would be kind to Burns. But, of course, she would; there was no end to her understanding where volunteers were concerned. Doctor Henry had said that the company were just living on Nuala's enthusiasm; there was something in it too. Burns had grown above that; he was an influence for strength himself now. He is getting more from her than the others, he thought, and in the cold morning he shivered; his wet clothes clung to him. Strange she had not answered, he thought, as the gravel sounded again and again, and Burns' voice said 'Nuala.'

Nuala could scarcely be away from home, The

Knife mused. There was just the merest chance she might have stayed with Nora Dan Sweeney; the very thinnest chance, he thought. It was foolish of Burns to go on pegging at the window; Nuala would have been up first shot, as awake and alert as though a night's sleep was ended. The Knife turned back towards the house, and he heard Burns' tramp on the gravel. Burns was going into the kitchen. The Knife halted, and his eye remained riveted on Nuala's window; the curtains were dented as only a grip could break their free outline as they swayed in the breeze. Somebody was peering out. 'That's not like you, Nuala,' The Knife thought. 'It's not like you,' he added, half aloud, wholly awake now. He glanced quickly at the kitchen door; Burns was disappearing into the kitchen; The Knife stood stock-still among the trees.

Silence: drops of rain pelted down from the softly stirring branches; the window curtains in Nuala's room were swinging free; the kitchen door was shut again. The Knife edged closer under the shelter of a tree and waited; he had a revolver in each hand now, and he wondered dimly when he had drawn them.

Nuala may have been in the kitchen; she may not have been at home at all. Burns is wetting the tea; perhaps he had been genuinely hungry; it sometimes happens that a man thinks he's hungry when he's tired, The Knife mused. He glanced at his guns, and shoved one back in his holster, toyed with the butt of it, and then drew it again. He got down on one knee, and remained rigid, his eyes on the kitchen door. After a few minutes his gaze went back to Nuala's room, and from there to the path to the tree that ran an arm across to her window. He crept cautiously across, sheathed one gun, and with the other in his hand he swarmed up the tree. He did it easily, for he knew this tree well, and had often done just this trick. When he came near the level of the sill he paused to secure a good foothold, and then with one swift movement his head was in the open window, and his revolver was keeping the curtains aside.

The room was empty; the bed had been slept in. Very cautiously he entered the room, pausing only to take off his boots before making a step. He crept across to the bed, and put his hand in under the crumpled clothes; there was warmth there yet. He crawled to the bedroom door, and opened it gently, and then wriggled out in the corridor. Everything was silent. The Knife nodded to himself, and the puzzle that had been in his thoughts was solved; something was wrong; something was very wrong. He had heard of the 'sit down' raid before. Sometime in the night – and not so many hours ago either, he decided, remembering Nuala's bed – a party had entered Montgomerys and had taken possession; Burns had walked into the trap.

Doubtless Nuala was downstairs: Nuala would not cry out when Burns came in, nor even while he was pegging gravel at the window. She would have known that a cry could not have saved him then. He could picture her down there, blazing with scorn and anger. We'll see, my girl, he thought, fiercely in earnest now.

Silence. If only some of them would talk; he must get some understanding of the situation. He waited; outside a cock crowed; he heard a dog bark. 'Were you alone?' the voice came sharply from the kitchen.

'You are getting worried, Major,' he heard Burns say.

Nuala is in the kitchen, The Knife decided, hearing the exaltation in Burns' voice. He was glad that Burns had the strength that playing up before Nuala would give him. Burns had never been regarded by The Knife as naturally brave; he had learned that much of him as a boy, but Burns was a great builder and organiser, and The Knife had come to respect him. His concern now was for Burns; there had always been an anxiety that Burns might find it hard to stand the test of being closely up against it, and in the days since the police hunt had become dangerous, The Knife had grown to like James Burns. Nuala's presence would sustain James through any test, he thought.

But what was to be done?

He crawled quickly across the corridor, his boots in his hand. He must first get clear of Nuala's room, for the window might be used again as a look-out. He entered the room opposite, and after a look round, turned to listen, lying on the floor with his head out the door.

'The best thing for you, my man, is to cough up your story; you are for the rope, I fancy, caught in arms like this. Where are your pals?'

'There's thousands of them outside,' Burns said.

'I hope so; a relief party arrives soon, and they will be interested in these friends of yours outside.'

'There are no friends of mine outside,' James said.

'A man that can't tell the truth that it is to his own interest to tell deserves to choke,' a voice said.

'Take the old man and the girl as hostages, and search the grounds.'

'Come on, old chap, move. Get up, miss.'

'I will not,' Nuala said promptly.

'We will carry you.'

'Don't you dare lay a finger on me.'

'Well, do with the old man.'

There was a noise of a scuffle in the kitchen.

'You coward!' it was Nuala's voice.

'Make me your hostage,' Burns said.

'You're for the hangman certain, and we must not cheat him. Drag the old man along.'

A scuffle. 'By Gad, he has the strength of ten,' a voice said. 'I say, old man, I hate to hurt you, have sense and walk.'

'I'm not afraid to go out,' Godfrey Dhu bellowed. 'I'm not feart, but you'll not skulk behind me. I never dodged behind another, and no man will hide behind me unless I wish it.'

A violent crash in the kitchen, and a rush of air; voices outside; the old man had been rushed out.

'Go upstairs and keep a look-out,' a voice ordered.

The Knife got up quickly to his feet within the room opposite Nuala's. A step sounded on the stairs, it came along the corridor, and The Knife saw the figure enter the bedroom.

A bound and the thud of a revolver butt on an unprotected head. The Knife eased the senseless policeman to the ground and listened; no new sound from the kitchen. He tied up the felled man, and went out quickly into the corridor, pulling on the policeman's topcoat as he walked. He went quickly down the stairs, and stepped into his boots at the foot. He was now in the hallway, the kitchen was at the far end. As he came into the corridor, he became aware of a figure behind him. Where he stood the light was bad. He yawned, and sat down on the stairs.

'I wish to Christ we were out of this,' a voice said behind.

The Knife mumbled to himself. When he stole a glance the policeman behind was resting on the window, half asleep. Something outside caught his eye, and he got to his feet, turned on his heel, and took a couple of quick steps towards the door. The Knife strode after him, and was into the kitchen at his heels. There were four men in the kitchen. Burns stood, handcuffed, near Nuala, who sat very erect in a chair.

'It's all over with you boys,' The Knife said. 'Put them up,' he added sharply.

The policeman in front halted, but one of The Knife's guns jabbed into his back, and he promptly raised his hands, and the others, feeling that their colleague at the door must have a knowledge of things beyond them, followed his example.

'Collect the guns, you, Nuala; get these handcuffs off, sergeant,' The Knife said. 'I don't wish to kill any more of you than has been killed this morning already,' he added, his gaze sweeping the policemen. 'Come on, crowd into the cellar,' The Knife ordered. 'You will be all right, I promise you; down those stairs.'

The man nearest the stairs moved slowly, and the

others followed; the sergeant hesitated, and then with a shrug followed the others. There were steps outside.

The Knife took Nuala to his side by a jerk of his head. 'How many are outside?'

'Eleven men, the D.I. one of them.'

'That's tough,' he said.

He gathered the revolvers and hurried across to the front window. The officer was within a few yards of the door. A hatchet lay on the window-sill; Godfrey Dhu had been chopping firewood the evening before. The Knife seized the hatchet and waited. The door opened gently and the officer entered. He was slightly in front of The Knife when the latter spoke.

'I'd hate to do it, unless . . . Hands up!'

The officer's hand leapt to his revolver, and the heel of the axe fell on his helmet. He sank without a sound.

'Quick, get his uniform off. I don't think he's dead really.' The Knife flung the policeman's great-coat and cap to Burns, and got quickly into the officer's uniform.

The Knife darted upstairs in a few bounds, and returned with the dazed policeman, who had almost regained consciousness.

The officer too was showing signs of life.

'There's none of them killed; that makes things easier. You tell the sergeant that I could have wiped them out, and didn't. If they lay a finger on my father's head or yours . . .'

'Go you two, leave them to me; I'll fly a signal from the big tree.'

They went out on the street, and walked slowly to the gate. Policemen showed up here and there among the trees, and a sergeant started across the green towards them; The Knife waved him back. Once down at the gate, they raced along under the shelter of a wall, and from there got into the trees on Billy White's farm.

Up in the slope they waited; they heard a whistle blow. The Knife started to his feet when shots rang out in the morning air, and remained motionless while the lorries purred in the distance. Burns watched them disappear across the brae, but The Knife's eyes were on the clump of trees. When a flag fluttered there, he slapped his thigh and chuckled.

'Come on, James, I want tea now.'

They hurried across the fields to get into their dug-out before folk stirred about on the mountain-side.

CHAPTER TWENTY-SIX

A ROUND-UP was in progress, and it was very dark in the dug-out. There was no fire, the chimney had been drawn inside and a sod of grass covered the opening. The entrance to the dug-out was on the bank of the river, and the men in getting in, had to wade through water up to their knees. There was silence too in the dug-out, men sat close together, breathing softly, listening intently. A huge round-up was in progress. Thousands of troops were sweeping the area, while aeroplanes circled overhead. Old Dan Shields had arranged everything outside, and he would come back with news as soon as everything was clear. So there was nothing to do but wait.

'Wish to Jesus I had them after me on the broad mountain where I had a chance,' one muttered.

'Hush,' James Burns said.

Silence again.

'They must be damn close or Dan would be back,' a voice whispered.

'Hush,' James Burns said again.

The raid had come suddenly; Burns and his column had only returned from an operation in the back country, where The Knife still lingered among the locals. In the morning they had gone up as usual to Dan Shields for breakfast, and it was the watchfulness of the old man that saved them from surprise. It had appeared unthinkable that a force could have crossed all the broken bridges and reached the heart of the mountain without warning. It had been done, however, and had not Dan been out searching for lost sheep, they would have been on the top of them all without detection. The men had scurried back into the dug-out, with Dan to seal them in, while Mary worked to remove trace of any men about the place.

'They came so damn direct it looks like knowing.'

'If we thought we were trapped it would be better to make a burst; I'd hate to be trapped like this.'

'I was trapped in a fall in a mine in Fifeshire,' a voice said softly, 'and I saw men go mad trying to lift the world off their backs. You could frighten yourselves in here; forget about them. Can't a man die if he has to, and we haven't. Bar they were led here we could not be discovered.'

'Hush,' James Burns said. 'Speak low.'

And then suddenly men ceased to breathe; there was a thud of steps overhead; more steps, and then silence.

Scattered shots near at hand, an explosion, and then silence.

'That was a mine,' Burns said.

'Let's go to sleep,' somebody suggested. 'They may camp there for days.'

'Pass round some water,' Burns said.

'With the daylight outside, we could strike a light,' someone suggested.

The luminous dial of Burns' watch shone in the dark. 'We're just an hour here,' he said.

'I wish I knew what the hell they were doing; for all we know . . .'

A chorused hush silenced the speaker. Steps again, and this time voices could be heard. Somebody chuckled.

'Get lying down and be as easy as you can,' Burns said. 'We just must wait.'

In the darkness there was a shuffling of feet and the soft thud of body against body.

'I think somebody should tell a story; bedtime stories for children.'

Maybe you'd rather have a song?'

'I hope Curran and The Knife don't walk into it,' one said.

'If they do that's our hope,' Burns said. 'The Knife will do something to pull them off.'

'Unless he was trapped first.'

'You couldn't trap The Knife, he has a sixth sense.'

'It gives me courage that he's outside.'

Again there was silence. There were many breaths in the darkness and there was a stiffness of limb in the breathers. Now and then someone asked how the time went. Somebody snored slightly, his neighbour elbowed him. The time dragged on.

'And there's people say life's short,' one grunted.

'I can't understand what's keeping Dan.'

'I was wonderin' too.'

'I've stopped wonderin'.'

'It's sure some good reason holds Dan.'

'It's a puzzle.'

'Give me a drink whoever is close.'

'What's the time now?'

'That watch's stopped. Let me hear it. Then time has stopped.'

'What time is it now?'

'There's something strange about all this; it must be near dark be this.'

'It is dark.'

'Then suppose one of us crawls out.'

'Where was the use in waiting at all if we don't wait for Dan Shields?'

'Let me open the look-out: I'll be careful.'

'In another half-hour,' Burns said, 'another half-hour.'

Silence again. A dog barked somewhere.

'I don't know that bark, it's not Dan's dog.'

Silence.

'What time is it now? Well that's the longest ten minutes.'

'They must have made a terribly direct rush.'

'Everybody must have been asleep farther back.'

'It's a wonder it missed Nuala.'

'You'll find Nora Dan was on the call somewhere.'

'What time is it now?'

'Another fifteen minutes.'

'Isn't it quare how time tightens, and everything tightens when a body has nothing to do but wait.'

'Couldn't we try it now?'

'There's no sense in letting waiting hurry a body.'

Silence.

'Surely it's half-past now?'

'It's not twenty minutes yet.'

'Whist, listen.'

'Here's Dan at last.'

'Whist.'

'It's a dog.'

'A police dog?'

'I'll lead the way out into the river,' Burns said sharply: 'cross straight to the far side and take cover each of you. Unless you're fired on, don't fire. No crowding. Are you all steady? Go in the order you are. All ready?'

'All ready.'

Burns drew in the covering to the entrance to the tunnel from the river, and stepped into the water. Only the sound of the gurgling stream. He crossed quickly and lay down behind the bruach. The others filed after him. All were silent.

'That's only a neighbour's dog, I know him.'

'There's something quare about Dan Shields, or is it my eyes?' one said.

'Three of you will come with me and creep forward. If there's anything doing we'll fall back this way: our retreat would be back of the old kiln,' Burns instructed; he led off quickly.

Across on the far side the dog barked.

'Shields' house.'

'That was the explosion,' Burns said. 'I'll get over to that clump of bushes,' he whispered. 'Cover the door.'

He dived into the bushes and signalled the others up. He pointed to the gable.

'Good God,' one gasped.

'I'll go in,' Burns said. 'If they're there I'll fire. They'll not get me silently with a bayonet. I'll fire. Cover the door.'

He dashed across the green.

He entered the ruin; he came out into the open

and signalled the others up, and hurried round to the gable.

The old man and woman were dead. They lay together on the gravel, his arm across her shoulder. On the street beside them was a pile of shirts. The shirts had told on them; two old people with a pile of shirts. And they wouldn't talk.

The others came up at a signal; somebody said 'Tans.' They all knelt.

'Let us build an altar and wake them here,' Burns said.

Sentries were placed and the others built a resting-place for Dan Shields and his wife at the gable of their cottage where they had fallen.

CHAPTER TWENTY-SEVEN

THERE was a clash between the people and a party of soldiers when Dan Shields and his wife were being buried in the old graveyard in the shadow of the derelict church. The whole native population of the Lagan was there, and the mountain folk had come down in torrents.

A strong force of military had surrounded the graveyard and Dan Sweeney was asked to tell the organisers of the procession that any attempt at inflaming the temper of the people would be suppressed; that there must be no meeting. The presence of the police and the military kept The Knife and Burns away; from the hillside they looked down on the scene in the distant valley.

'There must be no meeting, Nuala,' Dan Sweeney said, coming up with the warning from Major Price.

'There should have been no funeral,' Nuala said coldly.

'There'll be bloodshed if there's any attempt at talking to the people.'

'Then there will be bloodshed,' Nuala said.

Dan Sweeney flushed; he turned abruptly on his heels. He saw Phil Burns and hurried over.

'What on earth has happened Father John that he's not here?'

'I heard he was called off on a sick call.'

'Major Price has orders to stop any attempt at a demonstration; that girl of yours seems dead set on trouble, Godfrey Dhu.'

'She's likely to do a thing if she says it,' Godfrey Dhu said.

'Could you not get her to see sense?'

'I wouldn't like anything to happen to the girl,' Phil Burns said. 'It would be a pity.'

The crowd continued to pack into the graveyard.

'See the murder will be here if the soldiers close in on the thousands and thousands of people.'

'It will be worse than Cromwell at Drogheda,' Godfrey Dhu said.

Dan Sweeney grunted and turned hurriedly away. The officiating priest was waiting for the people to collect in the graveyard before beginning the service. Nuala was standing back beside a raised slab, Nora Dan Sweeney was beside her. Nora had crushed her way through with a message from Burns, and Nuala stooped to read it. It was an advice that the mood of the people should be used to increase the boycott of the police and soldiers, but that a risk of a stampede of the people must be avoided. Nuala had finished when Dan Sweeney came up with the priest.

'There must be no excuse given to the military to fire,' the priest said.

'Do you see Major Price down there, go down and threaten him.'

'Nonsense, woman, we have no control over him.'

Nuala stepped up on the slab and she was clearly visible to the whole throng. Heads went suddenly higher, and tension swept across the graveyard. Major Price was clearly visible too on a lorry by the gate.

'Major Price,' Nuala said. Her voice rang clearly across the breathing graveyard.

The major got to his feet. 'Madam,' he said, saluting.

'There is a tradition among us that murderers should not be present at the funeral of their victims. You are asked to withdraw.'

'I cannot argue with you, miss, about my orders,' the major said curtly, and sat down.

'What the devil do you mean?' Dan Sweeney demanded.

'Just what I said: it's our reply, and the funeral arrangements for this are the women's responsibility. You two get away now, I have to talk to Nora and the others.'

Nora Dan Sweeney touched her father on the arm. 'Trot along now like a good boy: you are far too respectable to have a quarrel with your daughter in public. Meantime, you might begin the rosary, Father, and please remain standing around here,' she said.

'Father Burns should have been here. I have no influence over them,' the officiating clergyman said.

'Better say the rosary, Father,' Nora Dan Sweeney suggested.

The priest began the rosary and thousands of voices murmured the responses. Up on the hillside, The Knife and James Burns and Curran heard the patter of the sounds.

'That's quare,' Curran said. 'I can still see the

coffin on the hearse, and that's the rosary for certain,' he decided, cupping his hand to the breeze.

'Nuala is up to something,' The Knife said. 'I think I know what she will do. I wonder who the old woman is who is being helped over the wall,' he added. 'I'll swear it's not just an old woman getting sick in the crowd, but a messenger coming through.'

'Most likely,' James Burns agreed.

They snuggled down in the heather and waited; the old woman came slowly down the lane from the graveyard.

'You'll see the difference when she gets in among the whins,' Curran said.

The old woman came into the shelter of the whins and kept straight on without change of gait.

'She's damned careful,' Curran commented.

The old woman came on and sat down near an old kiln.

'She's comin' no farther,' Burns said.

'She knows her ground well; it's Nora I'll swear. I can crawl down that drain and get up under the shelter so close that she can talk to me: she must fear someone is keeping an eye on her.' Burns nodded and The Knife darted off.

It was twenty minutes before The Knife was close enough to talk.

'Nora,' he called softly.

'How did you know me?' she asked.

'I just knew you when you popped over the wall.'

'Major Price called in French to a young lieutenant to keep the glasses on the old woman; they're looking. This is a likely enough place to rest. Can you hear me easily?'

'I can, fine.'

'Nuala is for refusing to have the bodies buried until the troops withdraw: they will stay, so will the crowd. That will keep them here till night and you can give them trouble getting back.'

'Price may think of that too, and hold hostages.'

'Nuala said nothing about that.'

'Tell her to think about that too. We will be ready, anyway, and . . .'

'Get away, Knife,' Nora called urgently.

'What is it?'

'There's a party of soldiers come out and they're heading this way.'

'Nora, get over into Bessie Mor's and get off that rig: let Bessie get into bed and tell her how you came down and all; she will play at being the old woman.'

'There's a policeman with them that would know me; he saw me in the graveyard.'

'Go into Bessie's and come out the back door: I'll be there.'

'But, Knife, you . . .'

'Do it now. Go on.'

Nora got to her feet. The Knife crept rapidly away under cover. He was scarcely at his post when Nora appeared.

'Did you explain to Bessie?'

'Bessie was watchin' and wonderin' who the old woman was that would come this way: she was getting into bed and the last I heard of her was thankin' God she had an attack of the wind and now it won't go to loss.'

She took The Knife's hand and chuckled.

'Go in that way and get into the drain behind the white rock.'

'Knife.'

'What?'

'Creep in front of me.'

'Go on or I'll give you a skelp.'

They flopped into the drain together.

'They must have come very quickly,' The Knife said, peeping out.

'You shouldn't have waited, Knife,' Nora said.

'Whist, woman.' He put an arm around her shoulders and drew her close. 'They're scatterin' around, searching.'

'It's that blasted peeler: he missed me maybe. He has an idea it's me, and maybe Bessie didn't play her part well.'

'Likely said too much. Go down cautiously, Nora; you'll get wet, but crawl on down that way; get under the briars and crawl.'

'And you?'

'I'll crawl too, when I see things clearer. And don't show up no matter what you hear.'

'Knife,' Nora said, grasping his arm.

'Go now, Nora, like a girl, quick.'

She dropped on her knees in the drain; very slowly she crawled under the briars. He watched her disappear. Then he crossed through the briars across the stream and where he mounted the bank his passage could clearly be seen.

The Knife was now badly off for cover: he crept along between low flags. The sun was in his favour and his clothes were grey, and he had wormed his way a good two hundred yards from the stream before any pursuer showed up. A soldier and a policeman came into view. They were higher up and came slowly. It was the soldier who first pointed to the broken brambles and he and the policeman hurried to the spot where Nora and The Knife had entered the stream.

The soldier turned to signal to his companions; the policeman was alone. He bent and examined the marks on the ditch. The Knife lay flat with part of his body sunk in a hollow out of which children at play had rolled a stone. He fixed the stock to his automatic pistol and trained it on the policeman. When he saw his helmet jerk up and his face turn quickly down the stream, he fired, and the policeman fell forward, hanging over the drain.

The Knife got to his feet and raced up the mountain in full view of the hurrying soldiers. The sun helped a lot and the first hurriedly fired shots, missed. He disappeared behind a bog bank and as he did so he heard shots from the right: Burns and Curran had now joined in and they had rifles.

The Knife went lower down, moving away from Curran and Burns and came into view of what was happening from between two boulders. The soldiers were running back to take cover among the stack yards, another party of military was hurrying out from the graveyard. The rifle fire from Burns and Curran was now farther to the right, and the movement of the soldiers was in that direction too. The policeman was being carried around Bessie Mor's gable. The Knife moved quickly from boulder to boulder, an old water track led back to the stream and he entered it and raced wildly down it.

'Nora,' he called, 'Nora.'

There was an answer from among the brambles.

He dived into the stream, tearing his way towards her and then turned and led the way back. He took her hand and jerked her into the new water track, and motioned her forward. One cheek was bleeding.

'Go as quickly as you can,' he whispered.

Firing was now more general. The stream had cut its way around a big rock, and after wriggling round that The Knife and Nora paused.

'They are gone the other way,' The Knife said; 'they are gone after Curran and Burns. I can get across to my rifle now. Are you hurt, Nora?'

'There is nothing wrong with me,' she said, 'nothing, Knife.' He wiped the blood from her cheek hurriedly, glanced sharply at the scratches and then smiled into her eyes.

'You're a splendid soldier,' he said.

'Let me come with you, Knife,' she urged.

'I'm going to travel very quickly,' he said. 'I'll try to pull them off Curran and Burns. You and Nuala come to the new dug-out to-night, wait for us there.'

He was off, and the girl continued to press her handkerchief to the cuts on her face; they still bled freely.

CHAPTER TWENTY-EIGHT

At the graveyard Phil Burns and Godfrey Dhu were arrested and put on a lorry as hostages, and they were only released when dawn came limping down from the hills. All night they had been herded here and there while the roads were being cleared. While the military had been ringed round the graveyard and hunting the hundreds of men, who, according to the official report, had attacked them from the hills, the two old men had remained close together, silent, observant of all that went on around them.

'You see what your sons bring on you,' the police inspector sympathised.

'I'm seeing what they'll bring on you,' Godfrey Dhu said.

'If we are attacked you'll be shot,' the inspector said.

'And if I'm shot The Knife will take you and grate you against some rasp-faced rock,' Godfrey Dhu said.

'A civil tongue might go a long way with you,' the policeman said.

'Same to you,' Godfrey Dhu countered.

'Man alive, what would I do without you,' Phil Burns whispered.

'I'm feart of my life,' Godfrey Dhu said, 'only I

hope I'm showing it as little as you. Could you not tell by me that I'm feart?'

'You look as scared as a cross bull a child would be threatenin'.'

'I wouldn't for the world they'd see it.'

'I'm trying to hide it myself too, but I daren't talk.'

'You're not feart, Phil.'

'Soul am I. 'Clare to me God, Godfrey, we're two bully old men,' Phil Burns decided.

At the barracks they were released.

'I'm sorry, old men,' Major Price said, 'and if you'll come inside I'll see if we can raise you a drink.'

'I suppose it's not just for the drink you took us,' Godfrey Dhu said.

'Well no.'

'Second thought hospitality is a poor thing. Come on, Phil.'

'I warn you you may be taken again; those sons of yours are unfair to you old men.'

'Ah, go to hell,' Godfrey Dhu said.

'He's lookin' after us,' Phil Burns whispered. 'Maybe he's switherin' about shootin'.'

'An' maybe he's switherin' about runnin' after us with a bottle; I could do with a swig.'

'He's still standin',' Phil Burns said.

Godfrey Dhu halted. 'Will you shut yer mouth; do you want us to shame ourselves now at the heel of it all? Me knees are knockin'.'

'Seo well, I won't say a word.'

'A plucky pair of old men,' Major Price said to those around him. 'It's a hell of a war this,' he added, turning away.

Godfrey Dhu went up with Phil Burns; their house was the nearest. Molly was in a panic; she burst into tears when she saw the two men approach.

'Bad luck to it for a country; if I had known where all this was leadin' devil a one belongin' to me would have lifted a finger.'

'Is it sorry we're back you are,' Godfrey Dhu quizzed.

'I was nearly out of me mind last night; a son of Barney the hills gave me the word.'

'A loose-tongued blather,' Godfrey Dhu said.

'I was certain sure they'd murder the two of you: I wouldn't go through what I went through last night for diamonds.'

'Are the boys all safe?'

'They're safe. And it was Nuala caused all the trouble. Father John heard it from Dan Sweeney. Dan says he's goin' to wash his hands of the whole business if women are goin' to be makin' war for men to fight; he'll just wash his hands of it.'

'He has a pair of hands would take a lot of washing,' Godfrey Dhu said.

'I'd like to see where the backin' would come from if Dan Sweeney pulled out.'

'It's me one worry that anyone belongin' to me comes within an ass's roar of him,' Phil Burns said.

'That's strange talk for you,' Molly protested.

'Get us a drop of tea, quick,' Phil grunted.

'James might have been shot too; they say the shootin' would deafen you; it was God saved him. I never thought things would turn out this way; couldn't some settlement be made that would give people peace? And the two calves are gone too,' she added.

'What happened to the calves?'

''Tis, like a fool, I let them down to Greggs: I thought I might as well have my share of the grass, for maybe I'm standin' me good share of the fightin'; and didn't a party of military sweep down on the place yesterday evening an' clear the cattle.'

'Divil far the cattle'll go; they can't fly. An' even if they did there's plenty cattle in the possession of the planters,' Godfrey Dhu said.

'Is it stolen cattle I'd let into my byre? Thank God I'm not that hard pushed,' Molly said.

'If any of mine's lifted, pets of the police will bear the burden then,' Godfrey Dhu said. 'And I'm maybe as little pushed as yourself.'

'No wonder Father John says the soul is going out of the movement; it'll soon be a question of grab, grab.'

'Father John's mother should be the last to encourage him to make sermons like the one he made when Swain's place was took over; you'd think it's the people are grabbers, not Swain.'

'You have enough anyway,' Molly Burns said.

'I have, an' I'm all for the grabbin' as you call it.'

'All I know is that it was a black day for this house that one of them lifted a hand to fight for the country. There's James now, and he can't lift a penny of the rates, and I suppose he'll lose the job altogether. Father John is out night and day, and there's people that criticise what he says off God's altar.'

'Sit up to the tay,' Phil Burns said. 'And if you

see a lorry passin', Molly, wave to it to come up: I had more peace on the lorry.'

The two men sat down to the tea; Molly went outside in a dudgeon.

'I have me own share of worry; what Dan Sweeney is aiming at I don't know, and he has so much influence with them boys of mine, it troubles me a lot.'

'James is a bully man now, a bully man. It would be a pity if anything tripped him up for he's making a grand race.'

Phil Burns saw Godfrey Dhu off and then went into the fields to work.

CHAPTER TWENTY-NINE

After some days James Burns ventured in home after dark. His father went outside to keep an eye on the road. He took his stand a little bit down the lane where he leaned against a fence, his head stretched forward, listening. Many a time he had rested thus, listening, while, inside, men slept or took council together.

A light, quick step came to his ear, a girl's step, a girl's step alone. Away over on the road there was the flash of a passing motor; over on the main road, so it carried no danger. Phil went over to the turf stack so that he could meet the visitor with an armful of turf, which would be a natural enough thing, and he would make a heavy tramp on the flags coming to the door if it was wise that James should retire to the room. The girl spoke as she came near, and Phil dropped the turf as he recognised Nuala's voice.

'It's cold for you out here,' she said.

'The little a body can do, he likes doing,' Phil said. Nuala touched his arm and went in, Phil went back to listen.

Inside, the Burns household were collected, and James was at the table with Curran and two others having tea. Molly Burns shook hands with Nuala. Shelia got up to get her a chair. James raised his hand in greeting. Nuala took a packet of despatches from her blouse and handed them to him.

'You would never guess who was here to see me,' Molly Burns fussed. 'I was just beginning to tell James about it; I suppose it's the Brigadier I should say, for indeed it's Brigadier Burns was out of his mouth every other word. Colonel Swain.'

'I know him; a cute, mean rascal,' Nuala said.

'Is it Colonel Swain? That man has more money to his name than would buy half the Lagan. I mind the time you daren't keep the road when he drove past. In here he came this morning, as simple as you like, and sits himself there in the corner. I didn't know whether I was on my head or my heels. "I hope Brigadier Burns is well," says he; me wondering where at all I'd say James was if he asked, for I thought maybe it's about the rates he was calling, for James hadn't been near him. "He's well, Colonel Swain," says I. "A remarkable man, a remarkable man," says he.'

'Oh, give us a chance, mother,' James interrupted.

A step in the street interrupted the speaker. Father John put his head in the door; Mrs. Burns blessed herself.

'The life left me; out in the darkness I thought you were a policeman, God forgive me.'

The priest greeted everybody, and sat down near Nuala.

'I was just tellin' them that Colonel Swain was in here to see Brigadier Burns if you please,' Molly said. 'You should hear the high opinion he has of James; the man is as sound an Irishman at heart as is in the country. He has different views from us, of course, but he's as simple a man as you'd meet.'

'It was some good reason made the old rascal call,' Nuala said seriously.

Molly Burns put her head in the air. 'It's not so easy for people to judge them they're never likely to come across,' she said.

'What was in his mind, did he say?' Father John inquired.

'Not a thing then, but good, had he to say about the boys. He said Brigadier Burns was respected by every man and woman that admired unselfish, upright ideals; you should hear the language of him. He said that part so often I put it in myself when he came to it one time.'

'It's easy for him to be polished, sitting there owning a townland, with the clans of Tirconaill in gardens around him,' Nuala said.

'No wonder for him to say there were ideas that would bring no credit to any movement beginning to arise; you shouldn't be bitter, Nuala, and if you put notions in them folks' heads the very things he fears will happen, and the movement will be disgraced. Them that never had more than the grass for a cow is aiming at making big folk of themselves by taking land off the Colonel, if you please. He didn't like to mention names, but he didn't contradict me when I said it's Limpy Donal Dhu is in the centre of any devilment that would be going on.'

'Donal would,' Father John cut in. 'He's just the kind of a nosey, sharp, greedy adventurer that would be early out for pickings.'

'There's fourteen of them in that pound of theirs;

how they live, God knows; it wouldn't be a bit wonder but if he felt Ireland was coming into her own he'd think he should get a bit more to live on,' Nuala defended.

'There will have to be a strong hand kept on folk like them,' Father John said. 'I hope everybody will set their face strong against any move in that direction. If not, it's all up; the respect of the world will be lost. The fight is not one for what can be grabbed by any man or class, it's a fight for ideals, a holy fight.'

'You would think it was the Colonel himself was talking,' Molly Burns said.

'Some of the boys often stay around Donal's – give him his due he'd share his last crust – and they may be putting ideas in folks' heads,' James said, turning away from the table.

'Indeed Colonel Swain knows about them staying round there, and he said he himself would be glad to give them hospitality.'

'The polished, cutè rascal,' Nuala said.

'It's a good job it's men, and not women, is leading Ireland these days,' Molly Burns said.

'Will there be replies to them despatches?' Nuala asked.

'There will be a verbal reply to one,' James said, opening the room door. Nuala followed him up in obedience to his signal.

'Don't let that old snake fool you,' Nuala said, coming quickly to Burns' side.

'We can't let people break loose and grab what they can lay hands on; they have broken into Swain's land.'

'And you are asked to beat them back into the steel jackets Cromwell put on them, James?'

She was standing straight and tall before him, and he swayed to touch her.

'And should I not, Nuala?'

'Hunt Swain,' she breathed into his face.

'I'll hunt him,' he said huskily. And then he seized her and covered her face with kisses. She made no protest and when he strained her towards him and staggered, she remained unresisting, unresponsive.

'I'm glad old Swain's villainy is checked,' she said when he desisted.

James frowned slightly. 'Oh that old fox; I had him sized.' His arms stirred to seize Nuala again, but after a second's pause he stooped over his despatches.

'Nuala,' he said without looking up.

'Please, James, let everything wait.'

Life leapt in James Burns, he swept her to him, and then abruptly flung her against the table.

'I'll make Swain jump,' he said later, striding across the room.

'It's a barefaced carry on,' Molly Burns said to herself. Hasn't she a face of brass, she thought, when Nuala came down out of the room.

CHAPTER THIRTY

LAND troubles were rising among the people themselves, and Sinn Fein courts were having a hard time holding back the servant men of the Lagan. A meeting of the people was called to meet the demand for land, and a man came down from Dublin, so that the case might be put before him. It was mountainy people mostly who were in attendance, with their womenfolk and girls and even youths. Servant men of the Lagan were there too. Godfrey Dhu was there, and Denis Freel and Phil Burns. Godfrey Dhu had driven round for the others, and they had gone off together.

The meeting was at an old castle on the mountainside.

'There was a day when there would be a quare rattle of drums at a meeting like this,' Phil Burns said.

'A whisper goes farther than drums these times,' Godfrey Dhu said.

'There was a big crowd when Father MacFadden was tried,' Denis Freel said.

There was a movement along the wall, and a man stood high above the people; he spoke in Gaelic, and his words came gushing. He spoke in English too, and his talk was about the inalienable rights of the nation, the will of the people, and the dawn of freedom. He was cheered when he sat down.

'Where do people like Hughie get all them words?' Denis Freel said. 'A man would never find place for quarter of them down with us. How does he keep memory of them?'

'He wasn't the sort of man that earnest people would be puttin' much heed in,' Phil Burns whispered. 'A nervous sort of a heady man. It's the big crowd made him talk.'

'It's a sound idea to get the like of him for a start. See Andy Mor over there; now Andy's like a curlew, frightened at everything that's going on. If it's something is to be done and he thinks Hughie's in it, he'll maybe think it safer than if a man of more nerve was leading it. Who's this?'

A quiet, blue-eyed, fair-skinned youth was now before the people.

'Owen Roe O'Neil had the rents paid to the Irish army; it's my opinion that rents should be paid to the Irish army to-day instead of us going beggin' across the world. A million pounds of a loan would be thought a lot of; there's millions going to the enemy from us. Let us cut it in two; forgive half entirely, and pay the other half to ourselves for our own fight. That's my idea.'

'There's sense in that,' Godfrey Dhu said. 'It's a pity he hadn't more words; it's just a bit too bare.'

Another speaker came before the people.

'We're in hen runs here, and there's land below belonging to us all. Are we going to let out on that land? Couldn't we make a committee of ourselves and arrange to go all out in a body and crop it? I'll go with my two horses, and I'll give over my share of the crops to the fightin' funds.'

The man that was up from Dublin came before the people. They applauded him, for he was a stranger, and he was known to have come from Dublin.

'It is only right to remind you that we are fighting for freedom, not for potatoes or oats, not to save a few pounds a year in rent, but to drive the British out of the country bag and baggage, and then the Irish Government will do justice to everybody. If rents are paid to the volunteers, there will be people that won't pay, and we'll be getting a bad name for making them pay; and if one stops every one will stop, and when we get free it won't be possible to get anybody to pay anything, and then won't the last condition be worse than the first? To tell people to pay nothing is easy; it is also very foolish. I'm sent down here to appeal to you all to stop making a scramble for what you can gather up out of the fight, but to go on fighting a good, clean fight for Irish freedom. The men of '16 didn't say: Come out with us and you'll pay no rent: Come out with us and you'll never need to pay anything. In God's name get down on the work, and fight for Ireland. If you turn the movement, as you are doing here, then we had better quit before we disgrace the heroes who died for the principle and ideas of Irish nationality.'

'I don't know what James Gallagher meant at all about running out on other people's land with his two horses,' a man said. 'It's some idea he has, for it's nothing mean James would do.'

Godfrey Dhu had his eye fixed on the wall and was silent.

'I suppose they know best in Dublin, they're smart men with learnin'; but it would be a good thing to stop the rent; it would make people feel there was strength and meaning in things,' a woman said.

A roar burst suddenly from the crowd. Nuala speaking excitedly had shown up unexpectedly over the top of the wall.

'Nuala, Nuala,' the crowd roared. She ducked from the cheering, and then slowly raised her head and looked out, calling over the throng; the sun was on her rusty hair, and her face was flooded with colour.

'I'm all against the Dublin man. I'm all for breaking the grip of the landlord when we have the power: I'm all for emptying down out of the hen runs, and I think James Gallagher shows himself a leader in Ireland from his talk. The talk that we heard from Dublin is the talk that Colonel Swain gave out when he was trying to convince us to keep the fence around his countryside safe from folk that was starving in the bog. It's not Irish talk; it's bailiff's talk.'

The Dublin man jumped on the wall beside Nuala. The crowd roared at him. He gesticulated wildly; the din grew louder. He turned appealingly to Nuala, but she stood rigid, her eyes on the hillside opposite where thatched cottages sparkled in the sun. The stranger stood down, and there was silence.

'Tell this man from Dublin to tell our Government up there that it's not only the English we want to drive out, we want to throw off all the burdens the English put on our backs,' she resumed. 'Let us drop the burdens first and we'll fight all the better for being free from them, and all the harder to make sure they will never be put back on us.' Cheer after cheer burst from the crowd as she disappeared.

'What she says is the God's truth,' Phil Burns said.

'The God's truth,' Denis Freel echoed.

James Burns came into view, and the crowd grew silent, heads were craned forward eagerly. The clash between Nuala and the Dublin man would be decided now.

'There's a Government in Dublin and we're pledged to it,' James Burns said. 'It is wrong, I think, in the way it looks at things. If we weaken it I suppose it would be bad. All I say is this: I'll not mix in these questions at all. If you don't pay rent nobody will touch you. And if you go out on the land it must be as James Gallagher says, a body of you, and there'll be a price fixed on what you grow for seed for the countryside, and them that works will get what comes in from the sale at a fixed price. You're free to pay rent or not: there's one thing you won't do, and that is take away from any man what he can work or what he works with.'

'It's a lead the people want,' Nuala said vehemently.

A horn sounded from the look-out on the hill-top, and the crowd turned away from the speakers. Burns and The Knife went off leisurely up the glen, and the crowd broke into hurrying groups.

'There was wisdom in what James said,' Denis Freel decided.

'There was wisdom in it,' Phil Burns scoffed. 'There's always wisdom in leaving things as they are.'

'I wouldn't give a spit for our chance if that's the mind of the leaders,' Godfrey Dhu said, 'not a spit.'

CHAPTER THIRTY-ONE

THE Orangemen had their meeting too. Sam Rowan was in the chair, and the hall was packed with gruff-spoken Orangemen.

'There's not much to say,' the chairman began, 'but what one has been saying here and another there is now to be said where there's more backing to it. Things are now out of our reach, and them that used to be our servant men are gettin' like to be our bosses. Colonel Swain's estate is in the hands of the mountainy people, and he can get no law against them. Gregg's place is a common. Wallace is left with one horse and what land he can work; and it wouldn't be surprising to find a rising of the whole servant men of the Lagan with the back country folk backing them. Colonel Swain is of opinion that we should press on the Government to give Home Rule to the part of the country where this uprising is going on, and that a bargain can be made that our property will be left to us if we let go of the political control we used to have. The Government will give Home Rule if we press for it. The question is, should we?

'Now I'll make me own mind clear to you all. One way and another I have been pulled into meetin' some of the people that's exciting the country. They're for going very far. Myself I wouldn't be a bit afraid of them no matter how far they went, but it's clear that people with more land than we have will lose some of it. The Government won't be able to put down the trouble. When they do things like killing Dan Shields they add to the anger against them; and rouse anger even in folk like me. These people's changed, they're strong minded and they'll go on and on. Now if the Government offers Home Rule it's expected that the leaders will take it, and that there will be jobs enough to satisfy all that have any backing. I'm not so sure how it will work; there's men won't be put under that way and it's doubtful whether them that can be bought have the power to overcome them that means their covenant stronger than the leaders mean theirs or we meant ours. Home Rule would maybe save us from a lot of trouble, and I suppose we can get it given if we think it's the thing to do.'

Sam sat down. Colonel Swain stood up.

'I am without a rood I can call me own; I have been told I have an estate somewhere else, if you please, and that I don't need this one. Now there is an assurance that the property of the Orangemen of the south will be safe, if all the offices under the Government are given to Sinn Feiners. There are meetings like this all over the country and if we agree, then Belfast will get the King himself to help us towards a solution. Can anybody see what Home Rule would work out like?'

'Can anybody not?' a farmer burst out angrily. 'It will mean us under a set of papishes; it will mean everything happening that we were to go through hell to prevent.'

'Nonsense,' a solicitor intervened. 'It is a step backward, of course, but all the things we used to beat up drums with won't happen. If we can hold our property you'll see that we can still call the tune. They will be in the Parliament, in the Police, in the Civil Service, but money and brains well used will give us the reins. But if we lose our property and we become penniless tramps in the country – well we lose everything then.'

'Why doesn't the Government put a firm man in control, a firm man.'

'It's too late now; the country is too excited and united. Home Rule will call them to feed out of our hands and do our biddin'.'

'If Home Rule is such a grand thing, what was all the fuss against it for?'

'Home Rule is our way of saving ourselves from worse. The Government has put it up to the leaders that if there's not strong guarantee that our property will be kept safe, they will face the world if necessary, but they will put down the disorder in Ireland.'

'Is the guarantee there?'

'There will be no Home Rule without it.'

'Well let them have Home Rule, and to hell with them.'

There were grunts of approval.

'Then stand up all that mean that.'

The whole hall stood up. Sam Rowan bowed slightly to Colonel Swain and then stepped away from the chair. The meeting was ended.

CHAPTER THIRTY-TWO

DAN SWEENEY and James Burns were together in Dan's room.

'The sooner you say it straight out the sooner we'll know where we are: is this damned girl runnin' the whole war? Is it for her you're fightin'?'

'It's not that way there's anything to talk about; what are the things that happened that shouldn't happen?'

'She's in everything, everything. You're all just her wee boys; it's her you're fightin' for, struttin' before her to make big fellows of yourselves. Why hell don't you marry her and have done with it?'

'Had you anything else to talk to me about?'

'There's the question of Swain's land and Gregg's; are you going to stop that?'

'I'm not.'

'So you're going to let your men take what they can lay hands on.'

'I'm of opinion that every man that's against this fight should get to hell out of the country.'

'That's her notions.'

'She maybe did a lot to make things clear.'

'And when you drive Swain and Gregg and the others out you'll have a dogs' fight to see who'll get the land; that will be fine.'

'It's a pity there's no scheme for dealin' with such things: in the meantime it's easy; we'll crop their lands in a body and make a war chest out of what we get.'

'That will help the country.'

'It's better than beggaring our friends, living on them.'

'I suppose you don't know that peace is comin'?'

'I don't.'

'Well it is; it's on the doorstep, and I don't want you to lose all you've earned by any foolishness now. Do you think Dublin will stand for what you're planning? You'll go back into the bogs in the bare-feet. I don't know what some of you chaps would do without watchin'. You have earned well of your country and you want to settle down in some good post. Well, your chance is coming. There's going to be peace.'

'Will it mean freedom?'

'It will; all the freedom that means anything. We'll have full control in our own country. We may as well see this straight and get it over. Home Rule is coming; and it's them that are sensible early will be the wisest.'

'What will it mean?'

'It will mean that all you boys will get the reward you deserve: the army will be in your hands; the police will be in your hands; parliament; every job in the country will be for your boys, and no one deserves better than you do, and you must not be a fool now.'

'It will be hard to satisfy the people now; they're expecting freedom.'

'And it's freedom they're getting. Our own army, police, parliament, money bags. Isn't that freedom? Everybody won't be able to get a good job, and them that's crushed out will yell, but they'll be put in their places.'

'The people believe it's for bigger things than that they were fighting.'

'The people my eye. Didn't I see them outside there burning tar barrels when I was made a J.P., and wasn't I cheered to the skies when I threw it back?'

'Will the land be taken from the planters, I mean the estates?'

'To be sure they'll be made sell.'

'Sell?'

'Is it grab you want?'

'The people expect the land for nothing.'

'An' what do you think we're going to have you boys in fine jobs in the army and police for, if it's not to keep notions like that down in the riff-raff.'

'What would be best for me to do?'

'A big job in the army; that's my advice. You have education, a name, and there'll be good pay.'

'I wonder what The Knife will say.'

'Say nothing to The Knife yet: only don't be driven into anything now that would come against you; if they're thinkin' of makin' peace in Dublin it's not what The Knife thinks will matter much, is it?'

'And they're going to accept Home Rule in Dublin?'

'They have promised that property will be safe, and the British have promised Home Rule; now you see where you were heading. You could lose all you were fightin' for. Could you marry that girl if you weren't in some big position do you think? Isn't it to marry her in the end you've been fightin'?'

'I want to make a home for her sure enough.'

'Well, now you've a chance to make it, get after things early.'

'How did you hear this? There's always roots to your talk.'

'There's root and branch in this; you play wise now and we'll travel far.'

'Parliament you're thinking of,' Burns said, taking up his hat. Dan Sweeney nodded, his gaze searching into Burns' eyes.

'You'll get there, the people'll carry you on their backs.'

'Always keep on their backs,' Dan Sweeney said with a grin. 'Watch how they treat them that fall off their backs under their feet. I'll take you through the back gate myself. Keep your mind closed now about all this.'

It was a breezy night with a drizzle of rain as Burns made his way out of the village across the wet fields.

'It would be a relief if we got a settlement,' he said to himself, and his mind brightened with thought of Nuala, who was back in the mountains nursing.

CHAPTER THIRTY-THREE

NUALA GODFREY DHU came down a mountain track. She was tired; she had been in a dug-out for days with a wounded man, and she had seen him safely packed into straw in a cart to be smuggled to a point where he would be driven to hospital. And she had seen him being dragged from the cart and flung into a military lorry.

There was a drizzle of rain and drops beaded on her hair and on the loose scarf around her throat. Her stride was free and quick, for she was in a hurry to get word through to Doctor Henry: his influence would possibly reach into the barracks to have the wounded man attended to: he was a little-known volunteer, and his life was in no other danger, she reflected.

James Burns saw her coming, and he noted only her free stride, the swing of her arms as she balanced herself on the stepping-stones across the stream; she was more alive than any living thing on the whole brae face, he thought, as she splashed across the last few yards. He waved to her, and her head jerked up sharply. She ran across the grass, and he had an impulse to dash towards her, but he delayed, feasting his eyes on her as she drew near. Her blouse was undone at the neck, and her bosom showed below the scarf. He stepped out to meet her; he put an arm around her shoulder, and looked down into her face.

'They have got poor Phil Molloy,' she said, and speaking quickly she gave him the details. They walked close together his arm still around her shoulders.

'It may be best for Phil; they can do nothing to him and he will get better attention.'

'I was hurrying to get word to Doctor Henry,' she said.

James frowned. 'What could he do?'

'He could see their doctor,' she said; 'I'll run on.'

'Come on in,' he urged.

They entered the cottage that for the moment served as a resting-place for the Column.

'The Knife has taken the lads into the Glen,' he said.

Nuala went up to the table and buttered herself a piece of bread.

'Sit down and I'll make tea,' Burns said.

Nuala got out of her damp coat. 'There should be a pair of stockings of Nora Dan Sweeney's here,' she said. She rummaged in The Knife's bag and got them. She sat down on an upturned box and put them on. James, in passing, stooped and slapped her on the bare leg.

'You are frozen cold,' he said.

'One gets cold when sleepy,' she said.

'Then tuck in and sleep,' he said.

'I'll rest till you make the tea.'

He piled clean straw in the corner, and she sank into it.

He sat on the box and touched her hand. 'The hand is warmer,' he said.

'I could doze off in a minute.'

'Then doze.'

The kettle boiled, spouting out water into the ashes. She lay stretched on the straw, her stockinged feet resting in the inside of his hat. He brought her tea in a cup, and sat beside her, holding the bread on a plate.

'Do you ever wish it was all over?' he asked her.

'I often wish we had peace,' she said.

'What kind of peace will they give us, do you think?'

'There can be only one kind of peace.'

'Men fight for a lot of reasons,' he said.

'They fight for freedom,' she said, rising slightly.

'I fight because you wish it,' Burns said.

'Oh, no,' she protested.

'But I do.'

She laid the cup aside; her face was very close to his. He dropped the plate and put his arms round her.

'Will you marry me, Nuala?' he whispered.

'I have no feeling for anybody that way,' she said.

'But I have feeling like that for you.'

'I have tried to feel that way,' she said: 'it was no good; it is no good.'

'But you must marry me.'

'What good would that be, James? I'm raw; that's how I think about myself: maybe I'll ripen: maybe I'll be ripe when you've won.' She tried to smile.

'I want you now.'

He put his arms under her knees, and lifted her across his legs.

'Where's the use, James? All this means nothing to me.'

'Peace is coming,' he said huskily. 'You must ripen now.'

'Peace is coming,' she said quickly.

'Aye: parliament, army, police, courts – everything will be ours, I know.'

She pushed his arms away and got to her feet. He locked his arms around her knees, and looked up into her face.

'And we will be among the bigwigs in the land,' he said.

'Are they going to let the people loose at last: is it that gives you hope . . .?'

He jerked her aside and got to his feet. 'The people: what do the people care about us? Shelter us if it is safe: give a bob if there's a collection: fight over a field when it's safe for them to steal it. . . . We all fight for something: I fight because I want you.'

He drew her to him, and kissed her, tore her blouse and kissed her breasts, her neck. . . . 'Now will you marry me?'

'James, can't you see, all this means nothing to me.'

'You won't marry me,' he said.

'Can't you see?'

They were both silent; she was gazing out of the window and a motor car passed; perhaps that was the Doctor.

'I had better get along to Doctor Henry's,' she said quietly.

'So that's it, that's what keeps you cold, is it?

An orange blossom you intend to be when you ripen. . . .'

She turned very slowly and faced him. 'James Burns, I'm not blind and I have tried to need you, and tried, and tried: I let you do what you did now and those other times because I was hoping . . . You remember that night in our barn; that was the first time you kissed me: it made me ill. I tell you I tried.'

'Made you sick; I made you sick, did I? Well, I won't make you sick any more.'

He flung on his bandolier, seized his rifle, and strode out.

CHAPTER THIRTY-FOUR

THAT evening The Knife got word that Burns was down in a country public-house, drunk. He hurried down for him, going alone so that none of the men might know. James was in the kitchen with a group of locals round him when The Knife entered.

'Ye'll have a drink, Knife,' Burns said: 'ye'll have a drink. I order ye to drink and ye'll drink. You'll bloody well drink: a glass: a glass of the best for The Knife, an' ye'll drink it, see? My orders.'

'I'll drink it,' The Knife said quietly; he gulped down the glass of whiskey. 'Now, we'll go,' he said, taking Burns' arm.

'Go: where to? Amn't I boss of the show? This pub is ours.'

'We had better go: this place is risky for you.'

'Risky? Do ye mean to insinuate: that's a good word; insinuate: I'm not drunk: I can say insinuate: you couldn't spell insinuate, Knife: is there a man in the house could spell insinuate? Not a man: there's where James Burns shines: brains and education. I'll see you all right, Knife. I'll see you all right.

'I wasn't treated fair, Knife: she didn't treat me fair: I wasn't treated fair.' He sat down on a chair and sobbed: 'I wasn't treated fair.'

'Come on, James, like a good man: it's not safe for you here.'

'Not safe for me here? What do you mean? I know you, Knife – it was you put it in her head, Knife: you're at the back of it all: I saw it happening: you think I'm not the man you are: you put her against me: and it's because of that bastard, Henry.'

'Pull yourself together, James, and come on.'

'Who're ye talkin' to, Knife? You take your orders from me, see! Get outside there, and do guard: that's your place: outside and do guard. I'll show her whose who round here: I let you all be big fellows and now I'm spit on. Get outside, do you hear?' He drew his revolver. 'Get outside.'

'What hell's coming over you, James?' The Knife asked.

'I'm through with your breed, do you understand? I'm through with your breed: I was only foolin'; just havin' my little bit of fun; now she can go to blazes: that's me: I can have my pick of them.'

'You're coming home with me, just now, Burns,' The Knife said quietly.

'Comin' home with you: think ye can trap a drunk man: I tell ye I'm through.'

A car drew up suddenly outside: The Knife bounded to the front door, revolver in hand; James Burns pulled at his holster, and staggered against a chair. Mary Burns and Father John got out of the car: The Knife stood in the shadow of the door and let them pass in. He went quietly out, and from the hill behind the public-house he watched James being helped into the car.

Next morning the papers were packed with peace

talk. James Burns got word out from Dan Sweeney that peace was certain. He lay in bed and thought about it, and as he thought he was glad to find himself looking back with indifference on his scene with Nuala: she was too almighty aloof anyway: he didn't want her any more: he would have the best of what was going; he was in with the right people for that. Damn lucky thing he hadn't put Dan Sweeney against him: she had been aiming at that all along; she had been driving him to one thing after another: lucky he hadn't shot Swain. He would have to keep an eye on her now: she would fasten on to somebody else.

Then there was The Knife; he had never really liked him: he was glad to be rid of the whole damn lot: he would hurry to Dublin and get well in once the truce came: meanwhile he would lie low.

When the truce did come he met The Knife in the village, but he remained in conversation with Father John, and passed without greeting. People had seen The Knife stop and they noticed the anger in him when James Burns went by without heed. That evening Burns went off to Dublin in a car that Colonel Swain loaned him, and he was still there when the treaty was signed.

CHAPTER THIRTY-FIVE

THE news had reached the Lagan. The Knife and Nuala were standing under a tree near the river, looking out over the plain. Fires were blazing, somewhere a drum was beating loudly. Flares were rocketing into the sky, and the glow over the village showed that tar barrels were being burned.

'I wouldn't take it too much to heart, Nuala; these things are all made by one or two, and the crowd is just glad to be free of the danger.'

'You don't believe that yourself, Knife. Those fires are going to get a grip; the crowd that's backing them are cleverer than us; soldiers never win against politicians; you are going to lose, Knife.'

'I just can't understand Burns. He was a good man, and I thought in earnest. I suppose he proposed to you.'

Nuala nodded.

'And you refused.'

Nuala nodded again.

'Well, that's that. What will Dublin do, I wonder?' mused The Knife.

'Dublin will be like this. You could get a grip of the Lagan to-morrow if you called on all to follow you and hunted the waverers out of the place, and took the working men of the Lagan and put them on the land, and the poor folk from the hills and let them out where they could live. Let Ireland loose and she will fight for her freedom; we are keeping her tied and asking her to fight manacled.'

'That's how the conquest was made, Nuala,' The Knife agreed. 'Kicked us out and set men down here that defended the Government because under it alone they held land.'

'If I were a man, Knife.'

'Yes, Nuala.'

She turned suddenly and rested against her brother's shoulder. 'Well, I'm not, Knife. We were just beginning to get dangerous; there will be no lead to them alone who would fight, the poor. The scramble for jobs will be on now. Poor Burns was off early.

'Knife?'

'Well, Nuala?'

'You remember how you and me used to dream of sweeping over the Lagan; the tramp of horses and the roar of people out of the bogs? We never dreamt of your becoming a great man, with money and importance, and the people being driven back into the bogs, sure we didn't, Knife?'

'We didn't, Nuala. Nor did we dream of these people of the bogs stamping over our faces.'

'You think that will come, Knife?'

'That's what I see.'

She shuddered. 'This is the peace of Dan Sweeney, of Father Burns, and of Molly Burns. Poor Molly. "People were laughing at me thinking that James' wildness was dragging me down; now they see there was sense in his wildness all along," she said to me at the chapel gate last Sunday.'

'Does she know that you refused James?'

Nuala smiled. 'Poor Molly Burns,' was all she said. 'Is that a fire at Curran's?' she asked sharply.

A blaze had shot up suddenly at the cottage on the side of the brae.

'That's Curran's house,' The Knife said.

'And that's Curran,' Nuala exclaimed, clapping her hands as the fire went out in scattered wisps of flame and showers of sparks. 'Good man, Curran.'

'Aye, and there goes another fire,' The Knife said, pointing to a jumping riot of fragments of flame.

'An' the big fire in Carrick Mor is down. I declare to God, Knife, the boys are out smashing this treachery. Race round and see what's happening.'

'I'll take the mare and do a tour,' he said. 'No surrender.'

'No surrender,' she called back.

CHAPTER THIRTY-SIX

NUALA was still standing on the bank of the river when Sam Rowan came along on the far side with a dog.

'I was over looking for you,' he said, halting.

Nuala said nothing.

'Have you won or lost?' he asked.

'We have lost, Sam. Won't you come over?' She moved down to the stepping-stones, and he came across.

'Our people's well satisfied,' he said simply, 'but they're wondering what backing the peace will get. Burns is away from you?'

'He is.'

'I suppose The Knife will fight very hard agin it?'

'He will be dead against it.'

'It will be terrible dangerous to fight agin this: I'll be very frightened for you if you go into a fight against this.'

'You were very good, Sam; we were unfair to you in some of the risks you ran, since you were not of our mind.'

'I don't know what's me mind: sometimes I'd rather go the whole way if you're going to suffer by the halt.'

'It's not right to look at it as if it was only me or

neighbours of yours were concerned; it's the country, Sam.'

'The country doesn't concern me, Nuala, but I'd hate terrible to have you hurt.

'Burns wanted to marry you,' he growled, after a pause.

'That's nothing for you to talk about,' she said.

'I never trusted him,' Sam continued.

'You never trusted him, Sam? Now what do you mean by that?'

'I was afraid he would fail you, and he has.'

'But it wasn't fighting for me he was.'

'To be sure it was,' Sam Rowan said.

She made a gesture of impatience.

'We were agin Home Rule in the Lagan; and then to save themselves Belfast let go of us. We had to plead to have it given to us in the end, and it came. I hate to think of myself with Burns agin you.'

'If Burns has the strength of the Orangemen of the Lagan behind him, then he'll do what poor Billy White tried to do: he'll end the Godfrey Dhus in the Lagan.'

'Poor Billy, he was a handful.'

'And the Lagan will be for Home Rule now?'

'They'll be for Home Rule.'

'Are you, Sam Rowan?'

'I may tell you straight, Nuala, that I'm like Burns this far: what I've done I've done for you, what I'll do it will be for you. And I'll do any damn thing I can for you.'

He turned slowly and walked away. When he was gone Nuala sat down on the bank and plucked the short grass thoughtfully. Suddenly she wept.

CHAPTER THIRTY-SEVEN

THE news that the Godfrey Dhus and the Burns family were 'black out' with each other went through the Lagan; James had come back from Dublin and talked freely. On Sunday the chapel was thronged. Never before had such a congregation assembled for second mass. The fires that had flashed out in the Lagan on the news that peace had been signed, had been trampled under the feet of angry youth. Many had cheered both acts. Sunday would bring the priest's mind, clear amid the confusion, and those who were uncertain what their final decision would be were excited at the conflict in themselves and between neighbours.

Father Burns was on the altar when the Godfrey Dhus arrived. They came with a group. There was Nuala, The Knife and Hugh, Curran, Breslin and some neighbours. Their appearance up the aisle set heads turning, very few whispers passed between the congregation. The Godfrey Dhus had only got to their seats when James Burns arrived. He was in uniform, and children got up in their seats to gaze at him. He came in with a big party of volunteers.

Mass began and the people knelt to pray. At the Gospel a string of men, who had arrived late, filed up the aisle; Nuala and The Knife exchanged glances, and when they sat down after the Gospel she leaned forward and buried her face in her hands. The Sanctus swept the congregation to their knees, and a hush charged with awe gripped the bowed throng, while the bell tinkled softly at the Elevation.

When the sounds died away and heads were straightened, fervour ebbed out of prayer, and here and there men and women yawned with the strain of waiting; something was going to happen in the chapel surely. There was a slight commotion while some person was taken out fainting.

Mass was finished and Father Burns turned to face his congregation. 'Say the Lord's Prayer and Hail Mary for . . .; the Lord's Prayer and Hail Mary for . . . Say the Lord's Prayer and Hail Mary in thanksgiving to Almighty God and His Blessed Mother for the divine blessing of freedom that has crowned our struggle.' And he began loudly himself to say the Our Father.

Nuala Godfrey Dhu got suddenly off her knees; The Knife, his beads balled in his fist, gazed steadily at the priest. Curran muttered where he sat, and people turned their heads to listen. The priest raised his voice for the Hail Mary and a section of the congregation thundered a response. Audible protests mingled with the prayers, and somewhere loud, angry words rang out.

The priest walked forward to the edge of the altar, and his eye swept the chapel; it avoided the Godfrey Dhus.

'For seven hundred years our fathers have fought and bled. Always they fought heroically, always they lost. The splendour of Benburb was drowned in the disaster of Scariff-Hollis; Beal-an-atha-buidhe was lost at Kinsale. And when Ireland lost, Ireland's enemies rejoiced. It has remained for our day to see victory wrested from our hereditary enemy, and the bravery of our soldiers, under God's blessing, crowned with success. Ireland is free. Rejoice, oh sons and daughters of Ireland! Be dismayed all ye enemies of our country in her day of destiny.'

In his excitement the priest was facing the Godfrey Dhus and his clenched fist pointed in their direction. There was silence in the chapel. The Knife was on his feet; his father stood up to let him pass, and remained standing. Those whose view he blocked stood up behind him, and the whole crowd was on its feet in a moment. The Knife went towards the altar; James Burns made a movement to leave his seat as The Knife approached and The Knife halted: James turned his face to the altar.

'It may not be enmity but stupidity and greed; it is surely hard to realise . . .' The Knife stepped in over the railing and went up the steps of the altar. 'If you dare . . . the priest thundered, raising his vestmented arm.

'I have little to say, but I'll say it,' The Knife said. 'I'm saying that the priest who makes use of the altar as Father Burns is making to-day is not fit to be a priest. Father Burns has made a platform of the altar. What more I have to say, I'll say as it suits me somewhere else.' He went into the sacristy.

'Did a Catholic ever dream a day would come . . .'

'Shut your mouth, and go on with the prayers.' It was Nuala.

'You, you shameful woman. . . .'

Godfrey Dhu was on his feet now.

'Shut up, you traitor,' Curran bellowed.

Violent arguments were spurting up through the aisle. A group of women came up to drag Nuala out of the chapel. Godfrey Dhu drew his open hand across the face of the leader, and she staggered back into the hands of her companions, dazed.

'Give them protection out of the chapel,' Father Burns called down to his brother. 'I can understand your anger, Catholic men and women, to see God's house so outraged, but let them depart in peace. Father forgive them,' he prayed, 'for they know not what they do.'

The Knife came back in through the sacristy, eight men tramped after him.

'It might be a good thing to wreck this chapel; you have fouled it, you skunk. If you don't get down now, and do it damn quick, I'll kick you off the altar.'

Father Burns trembled, and moistened his lips with his tongue. Slowly he went down the altar step and his voice sounded in the De Profundis. The people got on their knees and prayed. The Knife went back to his seat beside Nuala, and people avoided them on the way out.

CHAPTER THIRTY-EIGHT

THE congregation remained in the chapel yard. Godfrey Dhu was standing by the side of his trap, waiting for Hugh to bring round the horse, when Phil Burns came past. The two old men halted, and stood silent, face to face. And then Burns held out his hand, and Godfrey Dhu shook it; in all their lives they had never shaken hands before. Phil Burns blew his nose into his red handkerchief and went on.

A motor-car drove up, and Dan Sweeney arrived. There were two men in the car, and the tricolour was flying. A section of the crowd cheered. Nuala and The Knife were near their father, a group of young men strung around them.

'And here's Nora,' Nuala said, pointing to a cyclist. She came in the side gate and made her way to their side.

'Father McGinley preached hell's fire on us all. I did harm, for I started the *Soldiers' Song*; people were afraid of me on the way out. The choir all cleared except the youngsters, and I played the old harmonium as it never was played, and sang, and the kids backed me like men. I haven't seen father since, but I knew he was coming here, and I wanted to tell you. Did I do a lot of harm? It sounds terrible to behave like that in the chapel, but I just couldn't sit still, and there was the harmonium to my hand. When my head cleared I started a hymn.'

'We had ructions. Can't you see the way the crowd is?'

'They're not with the Burnses either,' Nora said.

'Here's old Cormac Mor; he's coming here. I'll die if old Cormac is an enemy,' Nuala declared.

'I'm going home to die,' Cormac said, leaning on his stick before Nuala – 'home to die. We're beat, mo veannacht doibh.'

'I can't bear to see old Cormac broken like that,' Nuala groaned; 'he was a great old man.'

There was a movement towards the gate; a man was on his feet in the motor-car, bareheaded. His opening remarks did not reach Godfrey Dhu, but voices called out challenges down by the gate. Blows were being struck.

Dan Sweeney stood up, and there was a hush.

'I'm your neighbour, you know me. I want to talk sense, to talk of what is for your good, to make clear to you things you should know. We have got our freedom.'

'We have not,' a voice challenged.

'Go away, you mug, you couldn't keep a seat in your trousers the best day ever you were.'

There was a loud laugh.

'The British soldiers are leaving the country; the R.I.C. are going.'

The crowd burst into cheers.

'All our lives we have suffered from the R.I.C. and now we are sacking the lot,' Dan continued. 'We will have our own parliament, the control of our own purse.'

'Just the way you control our purse, and make a bloomin' good livin' off us.'

'Even the vermin couldn't make a livin' off you, you skinny lout. There will be mad men and mad women here and there' – he emphasised mad women – 'and they will drag us back into war just for excitement, or burst. Let them marry, and maybe rearing a family will give them some sense. We are getting what we fought for, what Red Hugh led his armies to battle for. They failed, we've won. James Burns has done more for Tirconaill than Red Hugh and Godfrey: he has led us to victory.'

'Long live James Burns.'

'Long live a better man, The Knife.'

'The Knife is a good man, no man doubts that, but it's in the head his weakness is.' The Knife himself joined in the laugh. 'And there's that mad sister of his . . .'

'She's going over to the Orangemen,' a woman shouted. 'It's a wonder she never put on the trousers,' another called.

'I wouldn't go any further with that sort of talk,' The Knife said, and his voice went across the crowd.

'Keep your tongue off the girl,' voices called here and there.

'I have a madcap of my own . . .'

'Madcap or not, I'm here.' Nora scrambled up on the wall. 'You people think father is advising you for your good. He has been advising you all his life; he knows very well you are not going to get freedom, but he is. He'll be the big man, and James Burns will become a big fellow if he eats out of my father's hand. But you're big fools if you think you are getting your freedom. You'll pay your rents now or go to jail; you'll stick back in your wee pockets of land and starve. Maybe you'd get a cheaper passage to the States. The servant men of the Lagan will starve if the Orangemen don't want them.'

'There will be the police force open to them, and the army, and any good jobs in the country,' one of the men in the car shouted.

'You'll make policemen of the whole country,' Nora countered.

'They have betrayed you in Dublin . . .'

'Up, Collins!'

'They have sold you . . .'

'Up, Collins!'

'Drunken lot of sots.'

There was an angry roar from the crowd, and women rushed to pull the speaker down. The Knife lifted Nora down while a fierce struggle raged around. Dan Sweeney drove away in disgust and the meeting ended. The congregation, torn in factions, went home in groups. Here and there individuals walked, avoiding both sets of groups.

Nora Dan Sweeney went home with the Godfrey Dhus.

CHAPTER THIRTY-NINE

Doctor Henry came into Montgomerys while the excitement of the meeting was still alive. He had been to a patient near-by, and had parked his car under the trees in the avenue. The Doctor had been abroad for a few months, and the family had seen little of him.

'I can see that they've got you split all right,' the Doctor said, coming in on the floor. 'Well, we had to do it. When I came back from England cured of Orangeism, the King says, says he: "Doctor Henry is gone, and he's edging towards Fenianism, so we must get a new split over there. What have we in the basket to put them fighting over?" And you're fighting over what we are offering you out of the basket all right.'

'If I didn't know you had no joy in sayin' what you're sayin', the truth of it would make me very angry,' Nuala said. 'As it is it makes me . . .' Her voice trembled and she turned away.

'I take no joy out of it, and that's the truth,' the Doctor hastened to say. 'I tried to prepare you for it too. By the promise we had you could get no more than you've got, and the carry on in London didn't even promise this much.

'It's a tricky thing for the like of me to get talking

about men you all near worshipped,' the Doctor continued; 'but what I saw in London kind of made me ashamed, for in London I'm an Irishman. Still, mind you, they got as far as Home Rule could get.'

'They betrayed us,' Nora Dan Sweeney protested.

'You weren't fighting for Home Rule, so they betrayed that struggle sure enough,' Doctor Henry agreed. 'But there were lots of people with you that were only agitating for a Republic to see what kind of a bargain they could make, and Collins and Griffith were at the head of that section. They were helped to build up and get influence; the Press helped them for it was speaking for the same class. Now they're able to make what they'll call a "damn good bargain," and all the people who were looking to Home Rule for jobs will crowd round them, and they're going to get a great backing.'

'The volunteers will never betray the Republic,' Curran said.

'They won't believe Collins has betrayed it until it's too late,' Nuala said. 'Oh, why didn't we smother the salesmen by letting the people loose, and giving them something they could touch to defend.'

'No wonder we were betrayed,' Nora Dan Sweeney said bitterly, 'when there was nothing among them in London, only drink and rowdyism.'

'The betraying was done before ever they went to London,' Doctor Henry said. 'London was mostly play-acting for Collins and Griffith; getting the stage well set, with their threat of "Immediate and Terrible War," after they had agreed months ago.'

'Everything that could be raked up against them should be raked up,' Nora persisted.

'After the Parnell split,' Godfrey Dhu said, 'the country was as foul mouthed as any sewer; an' it's me opinion that that was nothing to what's going to happen this time. It's equal to you what you say about Collins and them, and what the truth is about their bargains. The bishops will cover them with their vestments. And wait till ye hear what they say about yourselves. There'll not be a girl of you but'll be in the family way in a month. Mark my words. I saw the Parnell split, and this will go as much deeper for dirt as the fight itself went above the Land League.'

'Father Burns spewed out on Nuala to-day,' Curran said.

'It's the like of him would talk,' Nora Dan Sweeney stormed. 'If a body was anyway obliging he'd be adventurous enough himself.'

'Aye, aye,' Godfrey Dhu said. 'There'll be little to choose between us in the stories, but they'll win.'

'They'll win,' Nuala declared, 'because there's nothing to show the people a difference. There's no way for the people to know what's the truth in the talk now, for we're doing nothing different from the others, and we did nothing different.'

A lorry load of armed men drove past; they fired shots in the air.

'And they're good lads,' The Knife said.

Nuala came out on the street with Doctor Henry and walked with him towards the car. When she halted he stood too.

'Won't you come down as far as the car with me?' he urged.

They walked in silence.

'There will be fighting again,' he said.

'It will be too late; it's now at once there's a chance, but there's too much confusion. Later there will be blows struck, but I can see no signal for renewing the struggle.'

'You are now farther away than ever, Nuala; you are walking in your sleep. Would you . . .?'

'Please, Doctor Henry, please.'

'All right, Nuala. And in the trouble that's coming I'm on your side too.'

'For the first time for centuries we had courage growing and glowing, rising as high as the blaze of excitement; in a short time we would have been great.' Nuala spoke softly. 'Now courage is broken, and excitement will be twisting into meanness. I just can't stand to picture what is coming; to let go of what I dreamt. I won't let go,' she added abruptly.

'You won't let go; that's just it, you won't let go,' the Doctor said. 'Well, there will be folk to hand to you too; maybe I'd have to rouse the Orangemen of the Lagan to save you yet. It could happen. And when it's all said and done, we're the only real fighters in Ireland.'

Nuala thought of Sam Rowan. 'There's a power in the Orangemen of the Lagan,' she agreed. 'But . . .'

'You're bewitching a man of good sound Orange stock: I'd better fly from the danger.' The Doctor tried to jest, but there was a drag in his step as he went towards his car.

CHAPTER FORTY

WHILE neighbourliness crashed around her, Molly Burns had risen into greatness in her townland. Now she was busy in the kitchen, preparing for a party. Mary had come out specially to help her for it was to be a swell affair. Dan Sweeney was coming; so were two priests, and a party that had come down from Dublin, and were staying at the hotel beyond. James would be there too, in his uniform with the decorations on it. Mary was bubbling with news and Molly on tiptoe with inquisitiveness.

'Did your father go back out to his work? Wouldn't you think, and all them people coming, he'd see there was water in at least? He's a bit of a trial, that man: there's not an enemy James or Father John has, but he has a civil word for.'

'There was terrible talk over him shaking hands with Godfrey Dhu; hadn't James the luck of God not to have married Nuala?'

'I never liked her; and it was plain to the world she was flinging herself at him; I don't know how under God he escaped her. The like of her be trying to trap famous men.'

'There's no knowing what James will be, according as they're making a fuss over him. Swain drove round in his car to call on him, and the daughter with him, if you please.'

'The daughter with him? It's little I thought that day'd come. But indeed that's a lie for me for I was always kind of seeing things since Father John went to college. Who under God is your father talking to? Look out.'

''Tis the postman; they're sitting down, if you please.'

'Call him in; that postman is not to be trusted. I hear he blows The Knife's horn everywhere he goes. I must speak to Father John about it. There's men that would be trustworthy that would welcome the job, picking out of your father he is. Call him in.'

'Father, your tea is ready,' Mary called.

Phil Burns waved his hand.

Molly was gazing out of the window. 'Now wouldn't he scald your heart; not a move out of him. Call him again, and the postman will take the hint and go. And put a drop of water on the tea, so your father won't see through it.'

'They have a paper in their hand and are looking at it.'

'I'll get Father John to get that man fired; your father is too innocent for these people. What kind of a clown is he anyway? Surely to God it's not a letter he's getting the postman to read for him.'

'He wouldn't do that,' Mary said, going out on the street again. 'Hoigh, father, your tea will be spoilt.'

The postman got to his feet.

'It's a wonder he had that much cuttin' in him,' Molly grumbled.

They came across the fields together.

'If he takes him into the house I'll say no more. Troth it's a wonder he didn't,' she commented, as the postman turned away.

Phil Burns came in.

'What rush of tea is on ye the day?' he asked.

'Mary and I were making a drop for ourselves,' Molly said. 'It's a heavy kind of a day.'

'Had the postman any news?' Mary asked.

'There's news; bad news. The fighting in Dublin is spreadin'. If that happens people might as well jump out with the spinks.'

'If there's people kicking up trouble against freedom, they should be clapped into jail and kept there; if there's people going to be that mad.'

Phil Burns drank his tea in silence.

'It's about time people put a hard face on them against them that's causin' the trouble; blackguards that's out for what they can grab. Word shouldn't be spoken to them.'

'There's people agin the settlement that will grab nothing for themselves; people with more brains than we have the name of havin'.'

'I'd like to know who would be darin' to have the brains or the education of Father John.'

'I wish to God Father John would do the things he's called on to do, and give the other things a miss.'

'If Father John heard you talking like that, he'd be mad.'

'That would be little to his credit.'

'You would think you take joy out of making a mock of the rest of us: here's the whole countryside cheering James, and if one says a word about him to you you'd think it's a mouthful of soot at you.'

'James is entitled to go for a job if he sees one, I suppose: I'd sooner a lot see him out in the drains there than doin' what he's doin'.'

'An' you make no secret of your mind either: I suppose that's what you were sayin' to the postman.'

Phil Burns got to his feet. 'People in this house seems firm in their mind to get what they can out of what's going. I'll stop nobody, but there'll be no more talk about any of these things on this floor, and if a friend of James or of Father John's says a hard word about a neighbour of mine, and especially agin the Godfrey Dhus, then if it was the Pope himself said it, out he'll go on the top of his head. An' there's tay for you,' he concluded.

Molly and Mary watched him cross the street and trudge back to his work in the fields.

'You'll never make a thing of him, never,' Molly said. 'Never. He doesn't want to rise one haeporth above them boys out there. There's the car; just as well he's out,' she decided, getting out of her apron to receive the visitors, who came with two lorries of soldiers and with the news that the Republicans were to be rounded up and put in jail. And Molly, with the great backing that was with James, felt very great that evening before her neighbours.

CHAPTER FORTY-ONE

Phil Burns on his way into the house for his dinner saw the new postman. He waited for him to come up.

'Is anything the matter with Patrick?' he asked.

'He wasn't clever enough, clever as he was; a despatch was found among his letters. He was lucky it went only the length of sacking.'

'An' there's a houseful of childer,' Phil sympathised.

'Our people have begun to move at last,' the postman went on; 'it's time. It was a grand sight to see Brigadier Burns leading his men out to sweep the Lagan this morning.'

Phil Burns said nothing.

'There's a guard on all the banks now; people has to call to the office for registered letters too, no good in raiding me.'

'I suppose your mind's at rest at night now, since they put a guard on the bank,' Phil said.

The postman looked up at the two-storey building in front of him, and then sharply at the man beside him. Yes, it's Phil Burns, he told himself; strange talk for a man like him. He remembered Brigadier Burns and Father Burns, and was silent.

'I hear the Godfrey Dhus ran like hares when Brigadier Burns drew on them.'

'When was this?'

'Down at their place this morning.'

'An' you tell me James was at Godfrey Dhu's?'

'He raided it; likely enough the bank money is about there.'

Molly saw them coming, and came out to meet them.

'Any news the day?' she asked eagerly.

'Brigadier Burns swept the whole countryside the day; there's not a Red left in the parish now but he'll have in the lorry.'

'Your dinner is on the table,' Molly said to Phil. He stooped over a tub to wash his hands.

'It was reported last night that The Knife and his mob were coming into the Glen, and Dan Sweeney sent word out for all the women to hide . . .'

'Clear, God's curse on you, clear to hell. And get you into the house, Molly.'

'Under God, Phil . . . Run, Eddie,' she pleaded.

The postman ran. Across the way Molly saw Sally Freel standing with her hands on her hips, listening.

'Fido, Fido,' Molly Burns called, and began pegging stones at the hens in the garden to make a commotion. 'Pitch a stone at them, Eddie,' she called to the hurrying postman, but he was too confused and alarmed to understand.

The dog raced into the garden and the hens flew about in fright. Molly glanced back; Phil had gone into the house. She called the dog to her, and walked back slowly, in her fine boots on a summer's day before her neighbours.

'Hoigh, Nelly,' Sally Freel called to one of her

children. 'Don't let the hens be pickin' at the barbed wire.' And she laughed loudly, and Molly Burns walked very slowly in home, her head up.

Phil was sitting at the head of the table, a half-peeled potato before him, his two arms resting on the table.

'Well, you made a show of yourself, and of us all at last,' she exploded, moving quickly from the door.

'I saw the day and I'd break every bone in that weed's body.' He had the knife and the potato in his hands now, and his hands shook violently. Molly paused.

'Isn't every sensible person in the country of one mind, except a few poor half-witted creatures,' she pleaded.

'I'd think very little of goin' into the town and chokin' Dan Sweeney at his own counter, the runt.'

'Dan has ways of hearin' things; I suppose it doesn't be all true.' The shaking hands were frightening Molly. 'Take a drink of milk,' she urged, 'and don't be making yourself excited. Sure after all what concern is it of ours, two old people? It's the young folk that have their lives to lead.'

'The son of mine that raids Godfrey Dhu's house . . .'

He got to his feet suddenly.

'Where under God are you going?'

'I'm going down to Godfrey Dhu's; if the young ones are fighting itself . . .' He was now so quiet-spoken and unsteady that Molly paused. She feared to speak; this was not anger. She moistened her lips with her tongue and watched him go out. After a moment she followed him; Sally Freel was coming up from the well with water.

'She has no right to be making a casan over our land,' she flared. 'I'll get that wired, so I will, and make her tramp round her own bogs. Why can't he be like another,' she added, watching her husband trudge slowly across the fields.

CHAPTER FORTY-TWO

Godfrey Dhu was alone in the kitchen when Phil Burns came in. The mattress of his bed lay ripped in the room door, and feathers were scattered over the floor. The delf off the dresser was piled on the floor, unbroken, and the stairs were wrecked. He turned when he heard the footsteps. Phil Burns stared at the wreckage, and then walked slowly across the floor until he was face to face with Godfrey Dhu.

'It's your house is ripped; it's my heart,' he said huskily.

'The cobbler's son that did it, the blackguard,' Godfrey Dhu said quickly.

'But my boy was the ringleader,' Phil Burns said sadly.

'It's Dan Sweeney was his downfall,' Godfrey Dhu said. 'It's only the mercy of God saved The Knife; that man's poison, and youngsters be foolish if they're in a hurry to get on.'

'I couldn't rest till I came down,' Phil Burns said, 'and it's little rest the sight gives.'

'I gave him a bit of a tongue when I came back from the river; it's then they done the tearin'.'

'We could fix the tick before the feathers get scattered,' Phil said, lifting a fistful.

'I was just going to begin on it,' Godfrey Dhu said.

'We'll get the most of them.' The two old men got on their knees among the feathers.

'Would you have a big needle and a piece of strong thread?' Phil Burns asked.

Godfrey Dhu got the needle: he knelt down at the door while he struggled to thread it. He shut one eye and held the needle high between him and the light.

'Brian was the same way,' Phil Burns said. 'He would have his tongue near over at his ear when he'd be threadin' a needle. Aye, aye,' he added, and sighed.

'Soul, but I've got it,' Godfrey Dhu announced, 'and it was just chance. I could see a midge in Aileach and I couldn't see print that would be as big as hen eggs.'

'I'm a good hand at sewing,' Phil Burns said.

'It's a thing I'm only very middlin' at,' Godfrey Dhu said, handing over the needle.

Sally Freel came softly to the door in bare feet, and halted on the street. She tiptoed away hurriedly. She stood under the shelter of the byre gable for a time and gazed around her. The curate's house drew her eyes, and a smile crept around her lips. She laughed a short laugh, settled the shawl on her head, and went quickly out a gap, hurrying across to Father Burns'.

CHAPTER FORTY-THREE

VISITORS were plentiful to Father Burns' house since the trouble began, and Mary was kept busy attending to them. At first each caller was ushered in to meet the priest himself, but now very few of them got past the kitchen. Mary collected their stories, and revelled in doing it. She became expert at the work, and her reports were models in their way; they were not a mere rehash of gossip, but sharp facts that the gossip revealed, and she herself often brought the reports to James. Mary played an important part in local espionage.

It surprised Mary that Sally Freel should come in, for in her troubles Sally always went to the parish priest. When Sally, therefore, walked in without knocking, Mary was for the moment frightened. The greatness of the Burns family was a structure around Mary, not a condition in herself.

'It's newens to see you,' Mary greeted.

'Not a bit wonder you'd be surprised to see me; and you have that much important business to look after a body'd hate to bother you without big reason. Nelly Ann says she sees you often.' Nelly Ann was a poor woman that for a part of the year went begging among her neighbours.

'Poor Nelly; she's badly able to tramp about now,

and it's the priest has the duty of keepin' her goin', not her poor neighbours,' Mary said seriously.

'Devil a thing is going on all over the country but poor Nelly does be havin' on her tongue,' Sally said. 'I wonder she doesn't deave your head.'

'One way or another most of what happens in a parish reaches the priests' ears,' Mary said.

'Is Father John in?' Sally asked.

'I'm afraid I heard his car goin' off,' Mary said, her head on one side.

'It's hard to get a priest at home these times, they have that much business to attend to; they say the only priest a body is sure of getting at home is the parish priest himself, he never bothers about a thing except his duties; he'll hear confessions any minute of the day.'

'Is it confession you were lookin' for?'

'Indeed an' now that you say it, it would be no harm for me if I did. But it's not that brought me in; I was just passin' and I thought it wasn't natural to pass a neighbour's door without a look in; neighbours is that strange now that if a body passes once, people puts meaning in it. An' if I go over to Godfrey Dhu's – an' I'm going over for some homespun that Nuala's giving me to make suits for the boys – people'll talk.'

'People's likely to talk if they see you takin' cloth out of Godfrey Dhu's; the childer is like enough to have it cast up to them: maybe callin' to the priest's ud take the appearance off it.'

'An' would people talk like that if they saw me coming out of Godfrey Dhu's with a bundle of cloth? It's at an auction Nuala bought it cheap.'

'There would be no doubt in people's minds the

Godfrey Dhus bought it cheap: them that goes into the house can't expect but they'll be thought to be gettin' something out of the loot.'

Sally got to her feet. 'Well, hoch, hoch, isn't that the foolishness. I hurried over because it was heavy to carry, and Denis said to me that if I ran down now your father would give me a hand back with it.'

'My father would?' Mary gasped.

'Aye; he's over there helping Godfrey Dhu to put things in order after the raid,' Sally said softly. 'God help them, and not as much sight between the two of them as'd thread a needle to mend the bed tick the Brigadier tore. You'd laugh at the pair of them,' she chuckled, walking out.

Mary gazed after her until she turned down the lane towards Godfrey Dhu's.

'I'll have to put out stories to give some other meaning to his goin' there,' she said, and she shook her fist at Sally Freel.

Farther down the lane Sally ducked down a drain and then took the near way back home.

'God help them,' she murmured, looking back towards Godfrey Dhu's; 'I wouldn't walk in on them two old creatures for the world.

'Amn't I to be pitied the way I be nippin' at them wans,' she sympathised with herself, darting a glance back at the curate's. 'I'll have to tell Denis it's over, seeing that poor girl of Nabla's I was,' she reflected. She pulled her shawl farther out on her head and hurried home.

CHAPTER FORTY-FOUR

Godfrey Dhu was often alone now about Montgomerys, for the Knife was again on the run, and Hugh was in jail. He had to attend the markets too. Nuala went through the fair to get to him in the sheep market. She was worried that day, for the news she was to have had of The Knife, who was away in the other end of the county, had not come to hand, and in its stead there was a rumour of further disaster and desertions. Her father was not to be seen, and she halted among the sheep to look around. There was a shooting gallery near by, and a number of Free State Tommies were among the group around it.

'The brazen-faced bitch . . .'

'She's rid of it this time anyway . . .'

'Your father was there a moment ago,' an old man said, coming to her side, 'he can't be far gone.'

'Cormac,' Nuala said eagerly; she had suddenly been afraid among them all.

'Aye, it's me,' he said. 'An' you're getting the cruel end of things, the cruel end.'

'Aren't people terrible . . .' Her voice shook, and she stopped speaking.

'Well, just look around you,' Cormac began calmly. 'There's poor old Daisy White, and with me own ears I heard them tellin' her in the post office that her pension will be cut off unless you're stoned out of the Lagan.

' "Stoned she ought to be," ' Daisy said.

'It's not what they say I mind, it's the change in themselves.'

'Come on, gentlemen, come on, gentlemen; three shots a penny. Well done, sir. Right in the centre where the Duke of Cork shot the lady. Turn the gun this way, sir; don't fire at the Orangemen's target.' There was a cheer from the crowd around the air-gun man, and in the midst of the cheer a scuffle, and the stand crashed into the street.

'Come on down here. I have a wee calf here that I'm herdin'. I might have left him at home for the devil a halfpenny there is, only I wanted a few shillings. Any word from The Knife?' Cormac whispered.

'I expected word the day, and it didn't come, he's still away.'

'They're beat, of course,' Cormac said. 'We're beat again.'

'We're beaten again,' Nuala agreed.

'I have as nice a hidin'-place . . . tell him,' Cormac said hurriedly.

A buyer came up and rapped the calf, and walked off.

'If you'll watch the calf for me here in this corner, I'll get your father,' Cormac suggested.

Nuala nodded, and smiled at him.

She sat down on a flag near Cormac's calf; she felt weary that day, and was alarmed at her sense of sadness. Had something happened The Knife?

'Are you sellin' the wee calf?' a voice said quietly

beside her, and she looked up with a flash of joy into the face of Sam Rowan.

'I am, and you must buy him,' she said. 'Cormac has gone looking for my father, and he wants to sell the calf. What's he worth?'

'This day you couldn't get more than four pound for the like of him: a baste of his size and make should go seven in a middlin' market.'

'When Cormac comes back, give seven for him, Sam; buy him for me. Clear now so he won't know. And mind you deliver him to me,' she warned.

Sam strolled away without a word, and Godfrey Dhu and Cormac came slowly across the fair.

'I thought maybe you'd like to come home with me,' Nuala said, getting to her feet.

'You needn't ha' worried about me, Nuala; there's as many old men of us in the fair as'd clear the town if we had to.'

'Soul would we, Godfrey Dhu, soul would we. But there's little to do, and less to see, here, and I'll be on my way back myself if I don't do something soon. If there's news from The Knife, and especially if he wants to lie up, I've a place and damn them, and he'd be safe.'

'You heard no rumour up the mountain, Cormac?'

'I heard millions of rumours, but they all came from that dunghill over there'; he nodded his head towards Dan Sweeney's. Nuala touched Cormac's arm, a barefooted youngster had come up behind them. 'I'll just try it out for another half-hour,' Cormac said abruptly. The Godfrey Dhus walked across the square.

'Some rumour must have reached Cormac about

The Knife, but if it was anything he knew he'd tell it.'

'As Cormac says, there's nothing but rumours,' Nuala said. 'I bought that wee calf of his,' she added.

'Well, there's grass enough for half a dozen like him,' Godfrey Dhu said, and in the drive home they picked up a couple of the neighbours, and the talk was of the market and the crops.

CHAPTER FORTY-FIVE

THAT night late a rat-tat came to Nuala's window, and she was on her feet in a second. It was dark outside, and she called softly.

'You don't know me,' the voice came back; 'old Cormac sent me.'

Nuala got into her overcoat, and raced down the stairs barefoot.

'What is it?' Godfrey Dhu called.

'A message from old Cormac.'

Nuala opened the door, and the figure of a girl came in out of the darkness outside into the kitchen, where the dim light before the statue of the Sacred Heart showed her face. She was a slip of a girl.

'What is it?' Nuala asked after a pause when she hoped the other would speak; she was conscious too of the silent, motionless figure of her father in his bedroom door.

'The Knife is badly, and wants a doctor.'

'Wounded?'

'No; pneumonia. Men carried him into our house from the hill, and Nora Dan Sweeney is with him.'

'Wonderful Nora,' Nuala said. 'I'll get a doctor,' she added, racing back up the stairs.

'Did you come all the way be yourself?' Godfrey Dhu said.

'There was no one else,' the girl said; 'my brother is back in the hills too.'

'Could you pull the rakings together and make a fire?' the old man said. 'It would help to warm you.'

'Come up here,' Nuala called to the girl. 'Get off your clothes, and get straight into bed. It's warm and you'll sleep. I'll get Doctor Henry,' she told her father. 'I'll go with him.'

'You'll let me know as soon as you can?' he said.

'I'll let you know,' she answered.

She pulled the door open, and went out. The trees were wedged into the darkness, and rain dripped on the gravel. The gravel path grated under her feet, and she walked erect, like a blind man, one hand outstretched for the wicket gate. The avenue was overladen with darkness, and again she walked rapidly in a straight line. The gravel here, dull with rain, was noiseless under her feet, but she got its feel for her guidance. She banged against the gate, and outside, the road, clear of the melting banks of darkness among the trees, traced a short grey streak.

She headed towards the village. The rain was behind her, and she walked quickly. Now that she was on her way she gave thought to the problem of discovering the Doctor. He was in the village, and the village was in the hands of the treatyites. They would be in the town; she must reach the Doctor without being detected; and she must get away without being followed.

She would never be able to get through the village without being halted. 'A dog couldn't move without a challenge,' was the news she had from the village. It would never do. She was still walking quickly. A flash of light from somewhere ahead: she was walking along by the high wall around Gregg's estate; she must not be caught there by a raiding party; she must not be seen by any chance car. The flash of light was wide amid the rain. There was no open field into which she could throw herself; she dived in among the brambles by the wayside and waited. The car came forward slowly, and went on its way, spluttering and coughing.

She came back out on the road; farther down the road the car was stopped, and there were voices in the breeze.

'I hope they don't raid home,' she thought, hurrying forward. And again suddenly a light flashed out in front: so close and so sudden was it that for a moment she stood still. She was in the sweep of the light, and in the silence she heard her heart beat. The light strained through the branches of a broken limb of a tree. And there is no sound of an engine, she thought, remaining stock-still now of purpose. The light went out, and she ducked in among the brambles.

She must get into the fields. Had the car behind gone far on, or was it in the darkness down the road? She darted across the roadway and scrambled over the high fence. The drop on the other side was a long one, so she let herself down until her fingers only had a hold, and then she let go. She landed among stones, and for a minute her knee hurt.

'I'll send Sam Rowan,' she told herself. 'I'll send Sam Rowan.'

She had not seen him since they met in the fair; his

servant man had taken down the calf. 'It's the only thing to do,' she murmured, 'the only thing to do.'

But it was dark among the fields, and there was no ribbon of grey to mark a pathway. Nuala made her way to the hedge, and then raced along it; the hedge would cut the back road that led past Sam's door. She could then work her way back.

A shower fell, and the rain, soft blobs of melted snow, thudded against her light overcoat.

'I must hurry,' she kept saying to herself, 'I must hurry.' She stumbled and fell, and her outflung hand banged against a rock. 'I must hurry,' she said, shaking the hand to soothe the pain.

Lights again in the roadway, a chain of light. A whole party had been lying along the road. Some good angel saved me, she thought, and then again, 'I must hurry, I must hurry.'

The fence loomed up sharply; she had reached the hedge at the back road. The search for a gap in the darkness would be a waste of time. She tried to crush through, but there were stakes within the fence; her knee came in contact with barbed wire, and she groaned.

'I must hurry,' she murmured, a catch in her voice. She went farther down. The hedge was broken here, and barbed wire took its place. It was tight, she could not squeeze through between the rows; it was high, and she could not climb over it. She discovered a post and climbed up; a strand of wire broke as she came down, and she fell into the road.

'I must hurry,' she thought, as she struggled to her feet. Rowan's dog barked; she knew the bark.

'Carabine,' she called softly, 'Carabine.' The dog

ceased until she pushed open the gate, then he came angrily towards her.

'Carabine,' she called again, 'Carabine.' The dog raced back and stood barking under a window. 'Carabine, Carabine,' Nuala called, coming forward.

'Lie down, Carabine,' a voice called, and Nuala's blood sang. She had been a bit afraid of that dog. 'Who's that?'

'It's me, Sam.'

'I thought it was,' she said. 'Carabine wouldn't tame for anybody else.' She came over to the window.

'The Doctor must be got for The Knife,' she said; 'they'd maybe not let me through to the town at this time; maybe they would, and follow us.'

'I'll get Doctor Henry,' Sam said, turning back from the window. She stood back from the slates; the spouting leaked, and she had been pelted with drops as she talked.

Carabine came along and licked her hand. There was a sound by the window. Sam was climbing through.

'They're all over the place,' she said, pointing to the motor lights.

'Aye; they're all over the place,' Sam Rowan said. 'I'll take a horse and a light, and go openly.'

She followed him towards the stable, his bulk clear against the white walk in front.

'They'll maybe raid here if they meet me,' he said.

'They maybe will,' she agreed.

'That'll be them already,' Sam said, hearing Carabine break out into new, angry barking.

Nuala was silent.

'I wouldn't be carin' for them to find you here,' Sam said.

There was a shot outside, and angrier barking from the dog.

'Come this way,' Sam said, holding out his hand to Nuala. He brought her in between the horses; she felt herself crushing against the side of one. After a moment's pause he took her up in his arms. 'Let yourself go with me,' he said; 'I'll drop you down, and you'll be safe.' A hoist, and then feet first she dropped down. Pause. 'It's a short drop,' he said. 'Catch the rope and try to lower yourself down.' Her feet touched earth. 'Are you all right, Nuala?' he called.

'I'm fine, Sam,' she said.

The gleam of light overhead was shut out; darkness, complete darkness. She shivered, and then suddenly her spirits rose; Sam Rowan's voice sounded softly above, speaking to a horse.

The dog barked again, and there were shots.

Sam's voice ceased to sound from among the horses. Silence except for the stamp of shod hoofs.

'. . . barks at any damn thing, a cat maybe,' she heard. 'I spoke to him half a dozen times; don't want him to waken everybody; barks half the night.'

'He says it's up at one of the horses he is,' a voice roared to somebody outside.

'He says we must raid the outhouses,' she heard next from the same voice.

'Well, raid away. Come in and get it over; it's worse on you fellows than on me.'

'I'm fed up,' the voice came clearer. 'This is a hunt after The Knife; he was seen being carried somewhere heading this way. The Brig. wants to get him, damned if we do. We're about fed up.'

'It seems strange to the like of me, hunting The Knife.'

'Better man, a damn sight, than them that's hunting him. If he's here, and I'm not asking you, tell him Big Micheal would help anyway he can, any time. Outside now, everybody.'

'I was thinking of goin' in to get something from the vet. for this horse of mine,' Sam said to Big Micheal.

'Just a minute,' Big Micheal advised. 'Outside everybody,' he ordered. 'I'll give you a lift in,' Big Micheal said. 'I'll talk the bastard into it.'

'I wonder if the vet. would rise?'

'Isn't a doctor as good as a vet?'

'Doctor Henry would give something,' Sam agreed.

'I'll give you a lift in; I'll talk the bastard into it,' Big Micheal said again.

Sam Rowan and Big Micheal were alone in the car; Big Micheal was driving.

'It's good of you, Sam,' Big Micheal said.

'A body hates to have a horse in pain,' Sam evaded.

'I'm a good man with horses, Sam; that's why I know.'

Silence.

'Is he badly hurt?'

'Hurt?'

'Aye, I saw the blood at your window.'

'No?' Sam gasped.

'Aye.'

'Then that wasn't a man's blood but a woman's,' Sam said, roused out of his caution.

'Oh, Jesus Christ,' Big Micheal groaned, slowing down; he brought the car to a standstill, and it purred softly.

'There was a day, and if blood was seen on Nuala!' he said; he slipped the car into gear, and went roaring down the road, and he said nothing to Sam Rowan when they parted at the Doctor's.

CHAPTER FORTY-SIX

FATHER BURNS fussed in and flung his hat on the kitchen table.

'They let him slip through their fingers again.'

'Well under God what cloud's over them,' Mary complained. 'The whole country will be thinking him more and more the hero after this. Wasn't it only a question of dashing at him? After all the trouble to get it fixed. What happened?'

'A rifle went off in the lorry.'

'There's people hand in glove with him around James. I'm getting frightened, it looks as if it wasn't to be.'

'Fiddlesticks. It would be the protection of the devil he'd have, and that's a poor shield.'

'I'll brain Sally Freel if she shows her face here to-morrow. I was sure the day would have been the end of the hunt, and put a different grin on some people's faces.'

'It's bad and very bad,' the priest agreed. 'And James is letting it worry him.'

Mary sighed. 'People's talkin',' she said; 'and talk travels.'

'It's not drink would come much against him, but people's getting on edge. James couldn't help seizing the cattle on Greggs, and he had no way of knowing whose cattle they were. He should have sent word, and people would have cleared the cattle and what he wanted to do would be done for him; now the looters is laughing because it's our own people's cattle was there, and the people that were caught are against us.'

'Sally Freel – I could brain her – came danderin' in here yesterday to say how little you can depend on people when the Glen ones were now cheerin' for The Knife.'

'And it was true for her; that blasted Knife. . . . And when we get him in a corner they let him slip. I don't know what James was thinking of. One thing anyway, The Knife's party is beat, and James may just as well go straight on with the job; no matter what enemies he makes let him get right with Gregg and the like, it's them have the influence.'

'You'd hate to have a fall out among ourselves now,' Mary said.

'Some people were only just hanging on to see what they could get, and when they see they're not going to get a hatful they'll round on us. Pure jealousy; that's all that was wrong all along.'

'People say The Knife could have got a higher job than James; that's what would madden a body. What learnin' had he compared to James? He couldn't put two words together, and James that could say the Latin like a priest.'

'When James turned down Nuala, The Knife got on his high horse. James should have caught The Knife long ago.'

'Where under God would he be now? He must be

run off his feet. How at all could we find out where he is?'

'Well, if anybody sees him they'll be in quick enough; I'll run over myself then.'

'Couldn't you give an intention in your mass? It would be too bad entirely if after batin' them all, The Knife would trip James up now.'

'The Knife will be caught; he was seen crossin' the road at the bridge.'

'I'll put a word out to Ann the master,' Mary said thoughtfully. 'It should be possible to get on his track again out that way. And if Doctor Henry's housekeeper could be seen.'

There was a rat-tat at the door.

'As true as heavens that's Sally Freel,' Mary said. 'I'll scald her.'

'Just play as cute as herself,' the priest advised. 'Be deep,' he said, disappearing out of the kitchen.

Mary opened the door, and Sally came softly in.

'I just ran in passin'. I hear yiz got him in the end, and do you know I was glad in a way he was caught; jail will be a rest for him.'

'If he's not in jail, it's not his fightin' saved him, but his runnin'. The hare they have a right to call him.'

'An' do you tell me he wasn't caught? Well amhaighdean, they say there was thousands after him. It must be feart they were to come close. Aren't you brave that's not scared of your life he'll come on James somewhere? A man that thousands won't jump on.'

'Were you wantin' anything?' Mary asked.

''Tis just to put you on your guard agin Annie

Nelly. What do you think she was sayin' at the wake in Darah, but that you gived her a pound note for tellin' that she saw young Denis Breen stealin' in home to see his mother the time she was sick; you mind he was drowned trying to swim the lake with the hunt after him. His mother wasn't there, but there's people'll tell it. And she's a woman there's a bad talan in.'

'Annie Nelly said that,' Mary gasped.

'People's sayin' nobody comes near the house to you but them that's carryin' stories; I hear there was a crowd of them was to go to the Bishop if the parish priest wouldn't do something.'

'An' who was at the back of all this?'

'You'd never know. And if this talk about you causing the death of Denis Breen gets a grip . . .' Sally shook her head ominously and turned towards the door.

Mary watched her off the street and then hurried in to Father John. He was asleep on the sofa and the uncorked whiskey bottle on the table beside him.

'God help me,' Mary said, 'if I haven't me own trial helping them all.' She put the bottle away and threw a rug across Father John's knees. Then she went out to the chapel and prayed.

CHAPTER FORTY-SEVEN

THE KNIFE had stolen into Doctor Henry's for a rest and now he was going off in the morning. Doctor Henry would drive out of his own garage with The Knife covered in the back of the car and race out to the beginning of the mountain track to Cormac's. After that it was a question of the broad mountain and good luck. The situation had improved; there had been desertions from the Free State Army, and restoring order had been resisted by people who had now new burdens to shoulder.

Nuala and Nora Dan Sweeney had crept in by the track from the river and had reached the Doctor's garden without detection, and with the Doctor and The Knife they were snugly settled in the former's study.

'I would not drag out the fight when you can't win,' the Doctor argued. 'You're beaten; it's no longer a fight, it's a hunt.'

'An' a hell of a hunt,' The Knife said. 'Still, I'll be easier in my mind when I get the heather under my feet.'

'I'm often sorry that my friends brought this on ye. We got them the treaty when we got the promise that our property would be safe; we couldn't hire a British general to do what Mulcahy is doing without all Ireland and America howling. Dick does it in the name of the bishops and the people, and Britain gets praised for standing aside. And what beats me is that lots of them that made it possible for Mulcahy to do our work believe they're fighting against us.'

'You'd be surprised how clear the mountainy folk are about it,' The Knife said, 'but they're just plain tired of fighting. If they had thought that giving in meant fighting the way it did, they would have been agin it. An' the poor lads in the army get no chance. "All that's going to remain true to the Republic, step this way; all that wants to desert, step to the rear." That was the order Owen O'Duffy gave when he was makin' the split in Dublin. And then the bishops are a proper lot of anti-Christs.'

'They brought you down, they'll do it again. You shoot some poor waster that is frightened or tempted into betraying you, and you let priests point out your men in the chapel yard, and have them led off to be murdered, and don't do a thing.'

'If my advice had been taken . . .' Nuala pointed out.

'I would shoot a priest, or for that matter a bishop spy, without a scruple,' The Knife said. 'But the result in the people's minds would be bad; that's the thing.'

'The next time,' Nuala said, 'the next time.'

'If you saw this over, and everybody at peace, and the hunt finished, you should be content to let the next generation take on that task,' the Doctor said.

'It won't take a generation to see what Mulcahy and his associates are doin', and there will be such fierce anger . . .'

'Put them up!'

The study door, vibrating with a bang, lurched open, and on the threshold was a cluster of men in uniform. Nora Dan Sweeney moaned.

'Get your hands up!' James Burns came forward into the room.

'Well, you've got me,' The Knife said, getting to his feet. 'I'm not armed,' he added.

'Get to your feet, all of you,' Burns ordered. Nuala sitting upright in her chair flashed scorn. 'Take the men outside,' Burns ordered.

'Look here . . .' The Knife began.

'Come on, you bastard,' one of the officers said, and he drove The Knife towards the door.

'James Burns, you wouldn't . . .' Nora began. 'Oh, Nuala, I can't be brave like you,' she exclaimed, flinging herself on Nuala.

'Dry the waterworks,' Burns said. 'You make me ill,' and he laughed. 'You're coming too,' he added.

'Thank God for that.' Nora brightened.

The Knife and the Doctor were put standing side by side in the corridor; the Doctor, his head stooped, was quite oblivious to the talk around him.

Burns and two officers were searching the rooms.

'Is this your room?' The Doctor nodded.

'And which is his? Is this your room, Knife?'

'Oh, go to hell.'

'Two double rooms; and very nice too.'

'Come on, you're coming with us,' Burns announced. 'Bundle them out,' he ordered.

The four prisoners were brought out into the hallway, and as they came out Sam Rowan was thrust in from the street.

'Found this man nosin' around; tryin' to sneak in the back.'

'A fine nest this. Oughtn't you to be ashamed of yourself; see what you've fallen to, Knife, nestin' with Orangemen.'

Doctor Henry's housekeeper came into the hall.

'You're not taking Doctor Henry. You're not taking Doctor Henry,' she protested. 'Father Burns said . . .'

James Burns drew a hand across her face, and she staggered back into the kitchen.

'Breslin saw her comin' out of the priest's house,' Sam said quietly to Doctor Henry, 'but he was late in coming to me.'

'Into the lorries,' Burns ordered. 'The girls in the second lorry.'

Nora Dan Sweeney dashed wildly towards the first lorry into which Doctor Henry was being hoisted. The Knife took her in his arms.

'Be brave, Nora,' he said. 'Be brave, you'll be all right.'

'And you, Knife?'

'I'll be all right,' he told her. 'Be brave.'

He released her, and she groped her way into the second lorry, and sat silent and dry-eyed beside Nuala on the way to jail.

CHAPTER FORTY-EIGHT

It was dark in the cell. A grey mist showed the heavily wired window, and the rustle of gas flame came from beyond the door. Outside too there was the jingle of keys and short bursts of song. Now and then a slide moved on the door, and a flashlight stabbed into the cell to light up the figure of a man, hung by the wrists from a hook in the roof. The Knife had now been hung up for hours, his toes just touching the ground, his weight swinging on his wrists. Consciousness hovered like sleep mocks an exhausted car driver, a thing of jerks and flashes.

The cell door opened and the noose was loosened. Landing on his feet The Knife staggered and a jailer prevented him from falling. He released himself and got against the wall.

'You're going back to the cell with the others,' the jailer said.

Consciousness was clearing. 'I hope you didn't disgrace yourselves doing the same to them.'

'I didn't know about this, Knife, I didn't know.'

'Well, I know all about it,' The Knife said.

'Can you walk?' a jailer asked.

'I can try. I can't.'

Members of the guard helped him up stone steps and down a corridor. A cell door was opened and he was helped in. He leaned against the wall and the guard after a pause withdrew. Doctor Henry and Sam Rowan rose from the floor and came to his side. The Knife held out his arms; the rope had dug a deep channel into his wrists.

'Very painful thing,' the Doctor said. 'Stretch him in the blankets, Sam.'

They stretched him out on the cell floor in a blanket.

'There was never such pins and needles,' The Knife groaned. Later, when the pain lessened, he drew himself up, sitting against the wall.

'Were you interfered with?'

'The butt of a rifle here and there, a jab of a bayonet in the thigh; just a few of them were nasty.'

'They can't hold you and Sam,' The Knife said.

'It was my housekeeper,' the Doctor said.

The Knife nodded. 'Father Burns got her to do it.'

'Well, when I get the length of Father Burns,' Doctor Henry said grimly.

'I hope the girls weren't hurt,' Sam said.

'They'll be either very nice to Nuala or they'll beat her head in with a rifle; and if they're nice to her, she'll be walking out the gate, with them standing to attention, before a week,' The Knife said.

'What can they do to you, Knife?' Sam asked earnestly.

'It's not very clear to me, Sam; there were no arms in the house, and I doubt whether anything else could be proved. They might make me a hostage.'

'That's what I'd be afraid of,' Doctor Henry said.

'It's the likeliest thing,' The Knife agreed.

'They must be terrible bitter agin you to crucify you like that.'

'Just some cronies of Burns; the most of them will be different.'

'Well, it's little I thought I'd be in jail under the Home Rule we pushed on ourselves,' Sam Rowan said. 'It's a bit of a joke.'

'They can't hold you,' The Knife said earnestly. 'I'll be easy in my mind when they dump you out. What's that?'

A mighty clamour broke out in the jail; a hammering that pervaded the whole building. Voices called and shots rang out, but the hammering went on.

'It's a puzzle,' Sam said.

Suddenly lime blistered on the wall of the cell and a brick shot in on the floor, followed by a shower of bricks as a hole was made in the wall. A lime-dusted, curly head was pushed through.

'You're the new prisoners?' the new-comer said.

The Knife nodded.

'We've been locked in for a week, and to-night was fixed for wrecking the jail. Creep through now, there's a passage all the way along; get to know the other animals in the zoo.'

'Be damn,' Sam said, grinning.

'Well, we may as well crawl along,' Doctor Henry said. 'It gets stranger and stranger,' he chuckled. 'Oh, my grandmother. Lead on, the Black Rowans.'

CHAPTER FORTY-NINE

'WELL, and how does the orange and green cell feel this morning?'

The prisoner who had been elected by his comrades to the position of officer in charge of prisoners leaned against the doorpost, and greeted The Knife, Sam Rowan, and Doctor Henry.

'The green part is tip-top,' The Knife said.

'The orange is no so bad either,' Sam Rowan said.

'And I, the sign of peace between them, feel peaceful,' the Doctor said. 'Won't you come in? There's much we have to learn.'

The officer in charge strolled in, and stretched himself on the floor.

'On an average, how many are killed per day in the prison? Such a ballyhoo of shots as was last night.'

'Last night was a bad night,' the officer agreed. 'But you get used to it. We are supposed to be in our cells at ten o'clock, but as you see the doors are smashed, and we can't be locked up, so the sentries fire up the wing; they really don't shoot to kill.'

'Ricochets off the wall,' Sam said, smiling. 'I'll be home early every night.'

'They can't keep Rowan or Doctor Henry in for long,' The Knife said. 'Are there many arrests like theirs?'

'If the locals have an edge on a man they can have

him held. You must teach us the *Boyne Water*, now that you're here.'

'I'll learn a Fenian song myself,' Doctor Henry said. 'I'll sing it at the hunt ball this year.'

'This landing is on fatigue duty this morning, scrubbing the floors and stairs and lavatories.'

'This landing,' Doctor Henry said. 'Then why are we not called in?'

'Well you are called in, and I've come to tell you. You'll find pail and mops outside.'

When the fatigue party was finished the doors to the yard were opened, and they trooped out into the ring. A tall, grey wall shut out the view of the world, but the sky was clear and blue overhead. A game of rounders was in progress, and there was much cheering and shouting.

'All this cheering and excitement is being worked up,' the Doctor commented. 'See the same few going from one corner to another and raising it; you would think it was around the hobby-horses they were; keeping up *morale*.'

A prisoner walked into the circle of the game and held up his hand; there was silence immediately.

'Classes are on,' he said, and withdrew. Groups of men here and there went back into the building.

'I suppose we couldn't look into the classes,' Doctor Henry said.

The Knife strolled across to the O.C., who signalled Doctor Henry and Sam Rowan to him.

'Yes, yes, you can go anywhere, into any class. We have engineering. Do you know the formula for blowing up bridges? A class for N.C.O.'s. Economics; there are a group of Communists here. Then there is a general school for those who want to improve their ordinary national school education. There's French, German, and, of course, Irish. There is a debate each night too, and now and then a concert.

'I think I'll take a hand in the game,' The Knife said.

'I'll nose around,' the Doctor decided. Sam went in with the Doctor.

A whistle call broke up the classes. Dinner was up; and the orderlies hurried to receive it, while the prisoners trooped back into their cells to get their mugs and plates ready.

'The engineering class had a close shave,' the Doctor yarned as they ate. 'I didn't know what was wrong when the talk switched. He was on the problem of how many cells connected in series would it take to put off a mine with three detonators, connected some way else, and all of a sudden he turned, and began to give us a talk about the analysis of soil and rotation of crops. I am puzzled as the devil how he got tipped off, for I heard nothing, and nobody turned a head. I gaped around, and there they were, two officers. They stood for a minute or two, then passed on, and he came back to his subject.'

'I had the best half-hour I ever had listening to some chap talking on some of the fights in the south. He said things to the Republicans about themselves that'd make me hit him if he said it in the Lagan,' Sam said. 'The man that supplied them spuds should be made eat them,' he added, after a pause.

'It's the tobacco that'll bother me; they say it's stopped often.'

He flung his pouch across to Sam. 'Fill your pipe, Sam, and rest yourself; we're on the rates now, and time doesn't matter.'

'O.C., O.C.,' was called from the gate.

'Keep that in your mind, Sam,' the Doctor advised. 'No man heeds anything the jailer says until the prisoner's O.C. relays the order. I picked that up on my rounds.'

'O.C., O.C.'

'Damn right to let the Johnny at the gate cool his heels. We're men of leisure and substance, and our after-dinner rest must not be disturbed. Give me the cloth, Knife, and I'll dry as you wash.'

'O.C.'

'There's a hell of a clatter outside,' Sam commented, twisting his long body round to look out the door.

'All hands out in the passage, and keep walkin'.'

'Lead the Orangemen into action, Sam,' the Doctor said, standing up. 'I had an uncle in the South Down militia, and another a drummer in Scarva.'

'I wonder what the devil's up,' the Knife said, piling the unwashed vessels into the dish.

On the way down they saw the O.C. standing inside a cell door, smoking. He smiled, and The Knife halted.

'We're ordered outside,' he said, 'and we're not ready to go out. I'm trying to gain time this way; the lads say I'm stuck in some cell playing chess, and they're looking for me.'

'You're not ready to go out?'

'No; we may be counted. You know your friends

well enough to decide whether you can tell them, but we're making a tunnel, and we can't get all the men out and washed just that quick. Another couple of minutes will do us.'

'All hands to the ground floor at the double,' somebody called.

'I'll chance it now,' the O.C. said, hurrying forward to the gate. 'What's all the row?' he asked, coming in front of the jailer.

'I'll have no more talk with you. Outside all. Get outside,' he ordered.

'Daddy, get a hatchet,' a youngster piped up.

'Get outside, get outside,' the military police ordered, swinging revolvers. The crowd kept marching to and fro, and nobody heeded the jailers.

With a rush a body of police appeared in the space before the gateway, their batons drawn.

'Close up and fold your arms,' the order rang out.

The prisoners packed the space inside the gate and stood still.

The gate was flung open and the policemen raced in. A man dropped under a baton; the crowd stood with folded arms.

'For Christ's sake, lads, get outside,' a policeman pleaded. 'Can't you go out, lads.'

The felled man was dragged back into a cell.

'Come on, use your batons,' the Governor ordered. He was a light, yellow-faced man, a-tremble with excitement.

'Get outside,' the police bellowed. 'Get outside,' they pleaded. Nobody stirred.

'I'll damn soon get you out,' the Governor stormed. 'Get back you,' he ordered the police.

The prisoners broke up into strolling groups, packing the floor with a moving, joking mass.

'To the gate, to the gate,' a voice called. Soldiers with fixed bayonets were now pouring in.

'We have won,' Doctor Henry said. 'He's bluffing.'

The soldiers drove towards the gate, and the prisoners folded arms. The Governor mopped his brow.

'Bring in the machine gun,' he ordered. The prisoners cheered.

'Come and see Dyer II. Won't mother be proud of me?' a voice mocked.

'Wait till I lay bare my bosom. I'm wearing my new shirt.'

The machine gun was mounted on the gate, the Governor whispered to the gunner. A burst of firing broke out, the bullets going clear through the window at the end of the wing.

'Stop that noise, stop that noise,' the crowd roared.

The firing stopped.

Out on the landing above a man appeared in his shirt and trousers. 'How the hell can a man sleep,' he bellowed. Gales of laughter rang out, the soldiers joining in lustily. The Governor walked into his office.

'Have you a match, Artillery?' one of the prisoners called to the machine gunner. 'As I must live, let me smoke.'

The gunner handed over a match; others moved forward to the gate. A soldier spotted a man he knew, and came eagerly over, handing in a box of cigarettes. The prisoners were strolling back and forward again, some returning to their cells.

Sam Rowan and Doctor Henry turned to face each other at the foot of the stairs.

'Orangemen couldn't beat these lads,' Doctor Henry said.

'No; but they would have bate the gunners,' Sam said. 'Unless they were Orangemen like us,' he added with a smile.

CHAPTER FIFTY

NEXT morning after breakfast the tussle with the Governor began in real earnest. The policemen passed the word round that the wing was going to be cleared, and that this time shooting would be used if necessary.

'Get back to your cells,' the O.C. ordered.

He came to talk to The Knife. 'You will go along this landing,' he said, 'and explain that we will crowd into the cells on the top floor, that will mean about six to a cell. They aim at dragging us out, one by one; six in a cell means that there can't come as many in as will drag six out. It will be a day's excitement, and it will tone up the jail. Explain to each cell on this side.'

The Knife went round on his mission. Later, with three Kerrymen for companions, they watched the military police crowd in.

'If they rake half a dozen cells at a time, we'll be in the first fight,' The Knife said.

They were. Eight policemen piled into their cell.

'Well, lads,' one of them announced, 'you're going out. Be damn but I'm not so sure,' he added. 'Who picked this cell? Well, let's get at it.' He took hold of Doctor Henry.

'Gotch threw me once,' the Doctor said, bracing himself.

A Kerryman threw his arms round the Doctor. 'We couldn't let Ulster be coerced,' he said.

'It's a terrible pity I don't know a song,' Doctor Henry said. 'That's how I feel.'

'Here he is,' a military policeman called in from the corridor. They made a pretence of dragging Doctor Henry from the cell until the officers passed, and then they stopped. A whistle sounded, the police withdrew. Prisoners pounded into the corridor cheering.

The O.C. came along to where The Knife was standing. 'They've got a new lot of thugs,' he said, 'and hosepipes. This crowd will rout us out or they'll hurt some of the youngsters. We'll fight the second landing, but I'll not let the youngsters get hosed. Volunteers for the second landing to meet the hosing.'

'Why not make it the top? The hose will be less effective there.'

'They'll begin on the second floor,' the O.C. said, 'and we may hold them there for a day. You needn't come, you know,' he added, turning to Doctor Henry and Sam.

'There's a kind of alliance between the Orangemen and Kerry,' Sam said.

'I wasn't going to volunteer,' one of the Kerrymen said, 'but I won't desert you.'

'You weren't going to volunteer,' the O.C. chuckled.

And now the fight became furious. A gust of water swept along the corridor. The cell doors were barred from the inside, but the central panel was driven in with axes and the nozzle of the hose pushed through. There was a tussle to deflect it; the crush of water was enough to send a man staggering. And in the end when the cell had been soaked, and the men inside deluged and redeluged, the door was driven in and the final tussle was on.

'No surrender,' Kerry challenged, when the water swept into the cell. Sam Rowan diving for the nozzle of the hose was struck with a gush of water in the face, and blinded for the moment.

'I see a rainbow,' one of the Kerrymen announced, during a short lull, while a struggle went on in the corridor with some person outside.

'This is where the Orangemen are,' a voice called. There was a sudden rush, and a bang of batons against bone. Sam Rowan struck out with his fists, and the Doctor with a swing of his leg took the feet from under an officer and splashed him into the water on the floor. A blow from the butt of a rifle dazed Sam. A Kerryman butted an officer with his head, and sprawled him across the Doctor's victim; then he too went down under a blow. The cell inmates were now rushed up the corridor, and hurled down the stairs, a relay dragging them, and flinging them outside. Each arrival was greeted with a cheer.

Numbed, exhausted, and sore, the hosed men staggered round the yard, some lay down in wet clothes. From the landing a prisoner looked down into the yard.

'Heigh, Tim, a cigarette,' Kerry called.

Cigarettes and matches came tumbling down. They were greeted with a cheer. A blanket came down.

'The very thing; Tim, pitch down all the blankets.' Blankets showered down into the yard and were shared out.

'Off with every stitch and into a dry blanket,' the Doctor ordered. Men pulled off their clothes and hung them up on the railings. Stark naked they raced round the ring. Somebody shouted 'Rounders, rounders!'

'Come on, Ulster,' Kerry challenged.

'Ulster strips for action,' the Doctor announced, discarding the blanket. 'Where's the ball?'

'There's no shortage of balls,' Kerry retorted, flinging the battered survivor of yesterday's match to Sam Rowan. And now amid the whirl of racing, naked bodies, and cheers, the task of clearing the wing went on.

CHAPTER FIFTY-ONE

WITH the fall of night the prisoners packed close together in a corner of the ring. There was no food; the door back to the wing was locked. The blankets of the top landing had now been emptied down, and the prisoners snuggled under them. Under cover of night sentries crept closer, and here and there conversations were begun.

'I read a book, *Convict 99*,' Sam Rowan said, 'and a man in it tore out the bars by putting strain on them in the centre, a blanket around two, and a stick to twist.' One of the Kerrymen helped him to experiment. 'We could tear the bars down,' Sam said, seeing the response to the pressure. 'Get half a dozen for it, and we'll flatten the yard fence.'

The other prisoners entered into the game, and a wild sing-song was struck up to deaden sound. The bars were swung down with a few mighty heaves. In the darkness a few prisoners raced across to the pile of farm carts and hand carts that were standing a little distance away, and dragged them into the yard. Bars on the windows into an unoccupied basement, which proved to be a carpenter's shop, were ripped aside, and a pile of light timbers was flung out. It lit easily, and before the jailers could discover what was on foot, a mighty fire was roaring in the ring, and cheers were drawing crowds round the jail.

'Home was never like this, yipp-ay-addy-ay-eh.'

'Three cheers for the moon,' a prisoner roared, pointing to the moon that had just then peeped over the jail roof; it was months since many of them had seen her.

They were heartily given.

'And three cheers for the wee stars,' an Ulster man demanded.

They were given.

'Did we get absolution?' a voice challenged, seeing the chaplain on the landing.

'No-o-o,' the crowd roared, and then 'Yes,' came louder, as their minds caught at the wag's meaning.

The chaplain withdrew hurriedly.

'That joke escaped me,' Doctor Henry said to Kerry.

'The priests here won't give any of us absolution when we go to confession; they were kiddin' him over the other kind of absolution we got this morning.'

'And why won't he give you absolution?'

'The anti-Christs in Maynooth made a new religion to back the Treaty, and because we won't give up the Republic or our religion, they won't let a priest near us except gligins like themselves.'

'Hush, hush.'

In the silence outside, voices could be heard singing hymns. Doctor Henry strained his ear to listen.

'That's the people singing hymns; friendly soldiers have told them there's murder going on. I have a wife and a mother out there among that crowd,' a Dublin man said.

'When they stop we will roar out a message. A word at a time. "We are all right." Ready now.' A prisoner got up on a box to conduct the broadcast.

And one by one the words of the message were roared out. From outside there came a cheer and then shots.

'They're scattering the crowd; cheer. Hip-hip-hip-hip.'

'Is there one of you called The Knife,' a prisoner asked quietly, and The Knife turned quickly.

'I am,' he said.

'Then come with me,' the speaker said, and moved across to a spot where the railings were unbroken. A Free State soldier was waiting. 'You had a sister in quod?'

'I have a sister in quod,' The Knife said.

'Had,' the soldier corrected. 'She walked out the gate in a rig I gave her, and with a pass too.'

The Knife sought the soldier's hand. 'Man alive, I'm glad,' he said.

'I'm a friend of Big Micheal,' the soldier explained. 'The other girl wouldn't go for fear she'd spoil it.'

'Could you take the other girl a note?' The Knife asked.

The soldier nodded. 'I'll be back in ten minutes,' he added.

The Knife wrote a note on a spare leaf in his prayer-book, and the soldier took it.

'Was he some person you knew?' Sam Rowan said, striding over.

'Nuala has escaped,' The Knife said.

'Nuala is out,' Sam said, looking up at the sky, and around at the prison. 'Man, Knife, am glad; man, but I'm glad.' He looked round for the Doctor, but he was in the middle of a chorus bawling at the top of his voice. Sam left it to The Knife to tell the Doctor and went for a stroll around the ring himself.

CHAPTER FIFTY-TWO

SAM ROWAN was called out and released without being permitted to return to the wing. Policemen came and removed his effects from the cell.

'I was thinking Sam couldn't be held long,' Doctor Henry said. 'We'll hear how things are at home now. The minister is a decent sort; it's easy for him for he has no friends among the jailers, and, though he won't act as postman, he'll write what a body asks him to say to anybody, and accept the reply to himself and retail it; that's the sort of sermons he preaches.'

'I was hopin' you'd be let out with Sam,' The Knife said.

'No; I'll not be let go with Sam,' the Doctor said. 'Not if I'm any judge of James Burns.'

'I'm not surprised at him,' The Knife said, 'and yet he could easily have been very different; he was getting over a lot of his weaknesses, and would have been a man by now.'

'He was only making a big man of himself before Nuala.'

'At first maybe,' agreed The Knife. 'But later there was good came out in him I never thought was there.'

'And now you'd see the dirt the devil wouldn't

have hoped to get stirring in him; and he has his brother behind him, and all this talk to make him a kind of saint in his own eyes, and whiskey to fire his own conceit. You'll see what Burns will come to.'

'I am kind of uneasy minded myself. It would be strange if a man could be full of fear and never know it was in himself. I was often scared for a minute, but I was never frightened so that I wouldn't face whatever was coming; but I'm kind of nervous in here.'

'Keep more in the open air, Knife, an' you'll never be so scared you couldn't face what you had to face.'

'I wish they would let you out, Dick; maybe part of what is wrong with me is that I've dragged you into something.'

'You didn't; an' I wouldn't have missed the jailing for anything. We'll soon know anyway, for now that Sam's let out, it shows they're working on us.'

'Maybe it's what they have in their minds is getting into me.'

'Could be,' the Doctor said, filling his pipe; 'it could be.'

'O.C., O.C.,' the guard on duty at the gate called.

'Maybe the parcels are going to be let in,' the Doctor suggested. 'Only for that little toff of a minister I'd be badly for tobacco by now.'

The Knife got up and glanced down over the railings; the O.C. was just approaching the Governor, who had a slip of paper in his hand. The former looked at it, and then glanced towards the top landing.

'Tell Doctor Henry he's wanted in the Governor's

office,' the O.C. called. The Knife nodded and went back into the cell.

'You're wanted now in the Governor's office. I'm right glad of it in a way, though I'll miss you like anything.'

The Doctor pulled at his pipe. 'Maybe I'm going. I suppose that Kerry bunch is out rounding? I'll maybe be back. With all the tunnel work, keep in the open air when you get a chance, Knife. Well, so long.'

'So long,' The Knife said, taking the Doctor's hand.

On the corridor he met the Kerry men.

'His Majesty the King has learned with some excitement that the great Doctor Henry had to associate with certain undesirables from Kerry, and he awaits me at the gate,' Doctor Henry said.

'Tell him he has gone a long way to winning over Kerry by kicking you out of his hotel. Bundle him out; bundle him out,' Kerry called.

They hoisted the Doctor on their shoulders and chaired him to the gate, other prisoners joining in.

'Speech, speech,' the crowd called.

'So long,' the Doctor said again, and he raised his hand to The Knife. 'So long, lads.'

The Knife was sitting on the floor of his cell making a cap out of a blanket when a cheer burst out at the gate. He ran out on the corridor; there was a milling going on down below, but the crowd was under his landing, and for a moment he could not see.

'It's Doctor Henry,' a prisoner called from the opposite landing. The Knife leaned over the rail and waited; again uneasiness gripped him. If only the Doctor were gone . . .

'Well, I'm back,' the Doctor said, stepping into the cell. The Knife shut the door, but there was a tap.

'It's me,' a voice said, and The Knife opened the door to admit the O.C.

'I'm back, you see,' the Doctor repeated.

'What happened?'

'Well, there's a court martial for myself and The Knife here,' he said. 'We were caught in possession of arms.'

'We were not,' The Knife said quickly.

'James Burns says we were,' Doctor Henry said. 'It's in the deposition. Somebody has been making a fuss about me, and I was taken out to sign a form of loyalty, to make things easier.'

'Burns is going lower and lower,' The Knife said disgustedly.

'It's funny, you know. It was damn funny outside. "Haven't we trouble enough and not to have you Orange bastards sticking your nose in," the Governor greeted me. He's a rare egg.'

'There's worse than him,' the O.C. said.

Doctor Henry nodded. 'Yes; there was a pasty rat beside him that kept his mouth shut, but it's in him the poison was. You should have heard the language of him when I was leaving.'

'Did he say when you'd be let out?' The Knife asked.

'He didn't say,' the Doctor said.

'There's men here for months with two or three papers signed,' the O.C. said.

The door swung open and Kerry came in breathless.

'They didn't let you out?' he said.

'They didn't let me out,' the Doctor said.

'Because . . .' Kerry hesitated, 'because you wouldn't sign the form.' It came quick in a sort of challenge.

'Because I wouldn't sign the form,' the Doctor agreed.

The Knife jerked himself upright. 'Is that just pig-headedness?' he demanded.

'The charge against you and me is a false one. I'm not getting out of a trap like that to make it easier to crush someone else; and it's not like you, Knife, to think I'd go. And I'm damned if I know if that's all that's holding me.'

Kerry and the O.C. withdrew quietly.

'No; you wouldn't draw out of a corner like that,' The Knife said thoughtfully.

'I'll see if I can't get into a game of rounders,' the Doctor said, going out. The Knife paced his cell alone.

CHAPTER FIFTY-THREE

THEY were both awake and talking quietly. Down below sentries paced to and fro, and outside the eternal 'Halt! Who goes there?' Snatches of song from among the military police, the crackle of gas on the landings, and then the jingle of keys at the gate.

'They're coming into the wing,' The Knife said.

The Doctor pulled quietly at his pipe.

The tramp of feet was heard ascending the stairs: up, up, up. And then along the corridor.

'Well, blast them, what about them?' The Knife said.

'Let them go to hell,' the Doctor said, laying his pipe aside.

The tramp ended, voices whispered in the corridor. The door was pushed open, and a flashlight dazzled the cell mates.

'Are you Doctor Henry?' the officer asked.

'I am.'

'Then get up and dress. And is this the other?' he asked, turning to the policeman. 'Get up you too. You may pack all your belongings, the Governor said.'

When the prisoners were ready, they were brought out on the corridor. A cell door opposite was ajar.

'Doctor Henry and The Knife,' a voice roared in the darkness. A sentry fired a shot.

'Good luck, Doctor Henry; good luck, Knife.' The prisoners tumbled out of bed and called greetings.

In the Governor's office the two prisoners were handcuffed and marched outside into the yard. They were put into a lorry which rapidly drove off.

'Well, what do you make of this?' Doctor Henry asked.

'I'll tell you when I see which turn we take at the cross. We're going back to our own county for that court martial,' he added.

'What I thought,' Doctor Henry agreed. 'That was a rare likeable bunch of fellows; all that shouting out of the cells and the firing of the sentries; queer kind of a picture. Keeping men like that in order by firing at them makes a man get notions.'

'Wait till you see the notions Burns has for us,' The Knife said.

The officer of the guard offered cigarettes.

'If there's any loose tobacco handy . . .' the Doctor ventured.

The officer drew up at a shop and knocked up the owner to get tobacco.

'And a drink wouldn't be out of the way,' the Doctor suggested. 'I've money.'

'And I'm supposed to have all your worldly goods in my possession,' the officer said, smiling.

The escort and prisoners got down on the road.

'I'll take off the handcuffs if you promise not to try to escape.'

'We promise nothing,' The Knife said.

'Then I'll not risk my neck. Short of that I'd do anything I can for you.'

'And short of that you can do nothing. And remember if you're in my firing party I promise to haunt you all your life.'

'You shouldn't talk like that even in jest,' the officer said.

'It's not in jest,' Doctor Henry assured him.

The officer gulped down his drink. 'We had better be going,' he said brusquely, and he was silent on the rest of the journey.

The prisoners were put in separate cells, and were not allowed out for exercise. They did not meet until they were brought together to the court martial.

'Stand to attention,' they were ordered.

'You go to hell,' The Knife said.

'Amen,' the Doctor clerked.

'You'll bloody well stand to attention before we're through,' an officer told them.

The Knife's eye was on the groups of officers assembled for the court martial. Burns was not present, but a door swung open, and he walked in, gorgeous in a new uniform.

'What the hell sort of a yarn is this of yours that you found guns in Doctor Henry's?' The Knife demanded.

'I found them,' Burns said.

'You're a liar.'

'Shut up, you bastard,' the officer of the escort said, pointing his gun at The Knife.

'Your time will come,' The Knife told him. 'The murder is not yet. This is the trial. See?'

'Read out the charge,' the President of the court ordered.

'So the tricky lawyer has ventured into uniform,' The Knife mocked. 'Well, you rat, would you dare sit on a court to try me.'

'He never joined the Orangemen,' a member of the court retorted.

'You ran too fast out of Belfast to have a chance to join anything; they made you adjutant because you were the only typist in the county. I'll smash your face if you dare go on with the farce of trying me.'

'Read the charge.'

The Knife took a stride forward.

'The court will take the evidence without any interruptions from you. Remove the prisoners.'

'Perhaps they will hang us in our absence too,' the Doctor said, when they were outside.

'I'm glad we're just right up close to it,' The Knife said. 'They'll shoot us, I see that. I never thought it before; did you know all along?'

'I had my ideas on the subject,' the Doctor said.

'If I could get one fist into the yellow blotched face of Glennon before I go.'

'It's on James Burns' windpipe I'd like to play a tune,' the Doctor said. 'Listen to them. 'Clare to my God they're makin' speeches.'

The guard stood around in silence. The Knife now gave his attention to them.

'I didn't expect to find you at a job like this,' he said to one.

The soldier looked very straight in front and was silent.

The door of the court room opened. 'Bring in the prisoners.'

The Knife and Doctor Henry tramped in.

'Doctor Henry and The Knife,' the President of the court began. He was a lawyer who had never felt a soldier among his fellows, but now he discovered himself playing a big role among them. 'You have been charged with . . .'

'Cut off the wind, William, you humbug,' The Knife interrupted. 'You're a nice bunch; some of you listening will please tell some of our lads some day that it is my wish to have this whole court hanged.'

'Shut up, you bastard; you're to be shot,' a nervous member of the court stormed.

'Splendid. In the morning?'

'You have been found guilty on the charge brought against you and the penalty is death; that is the sentence of the court, and I would advise you not to fool yourself into believing it will not be confirmed.'

'Of course it will be confirmed; and God help you lads when it does.'

'What do you mean by that?' the President of the court asked quickly.

'Wind up, William? I pity you,' The Knife mocked.

'You have heard the sentence of the court,' the President said; 'if there is anything you have to say that should be put in against the sentence . . .'

'That's up to you, for down you'll go.'

'Have you anything to say, Doctor Henry?'

'God pity you chaps, that's all I say. Between the Republicans and the Orangemen you'll be eaten alive; especially you, William.'

The other officers of the court joined in the laugh at the sudden fidgetiness of the President. The escort took the prisoners away, and they were put in the same cell.

'It's a pity we hadn't been sentenced long ago,' the Doctor said, when they were alone together. 'I must say I didn't enjoy solitary a bit.'

The Knife sat down on a bundle of blankets. 'I suppose you know they'll put us up against a wall?'

'I do, Knife; I've known that all along, in my bones like.'

'Your standing in will not save me, and you will go too.'

The Doctor struck a match and pulled at his pipe.

'And I do not want to die,' The Knife said, bounding to his feet. 'I do not want to die.'

'Me too; I'm too interested in myself at this minute to wish to say much.'

The Knife sat down on the floor and drew strokes on the boards with a nail.

CHAPTER FIFTY-FOUR

FATHER BURNS was chaplain to the troops. The Knife met him on his way to mass on Sunday; they passed without speaking. After mass the priest preached a sermon on preparation for a happy death, a simple, devout talk that was clear of the issues that had aroused anger against other sermons. The Knife was slightly puzzled, and his mind strayed occasionally from the discourse to puzzle out the change in the preacher. He recalled that sermon in the parish chapel, he was thinking of that day when the sermon ended, and it was still in his mind when he was going back to his cell. Again he passed Father Burns, and again he looked straight ahead and was silent.

Doctor Henry went out to a service that evening, and on his return he had news. There had been a great fuss in Unionist circles, but no hope had been held out. Without a declaration of loyalty to the new Government there could be no reprieve, and no person gave a second thought to any hope in that direction. The Knife would not, and Doctor Henry having refused before the court martial would not change under threat of execution. The minister would, of course, take out any verbal message that either prisoner had to transmit.

'I can't see much chance of escape,' The Knife

said, standing with his back to the cell door; 'none in fact.'

The Doctor nodded his agreement. 'It's just a question of squaring up to the idea of being killed; we may as well get that straight, dodging it or hoping would only weaken us, and make the final difficult.'

'Oh, I have no trouble about dying,' The Knife said. 'I feel right about it all, and at peace in that way. But I'll be mad as blazes about being blotted out. I can't understand how men shake hands with the firing party and say nice things; damned if I will.'

'That poor devil of a solicitor, the President of the court, is likely to have the jumps; I'm sure he thinks a Black Protestant is likely to come back with a lot of devils in him and wreck vengeance.'

'Burns will see ghosts if I can manage,' The Knife said.

'I think men shake hands with the firing party because they are just too busy within themselves to give heed, and since the other fellows wish to shake hands and all that, the prisoners do it to get clear of interruptions. Maybe we will be all involved inside ourselves too,' the Doctor suggested.

'I see Father Burns is chaplain here. I would like a real priest when it comes to dying; maybe Father Burns' sermon to-day was a hint that he has seen through the bishops.'

'Well, maybe; I scarcely think so. Dying Catholics get a lot of comfort from their religion,' Doctor Henry mused. 'I've seen them, man, in all kinds of corners in London, and it was wonderful. The priest rises to great heights in their minds then.'

'A priest would make dying much easier; this

district is a bad one though. I hear they have nearly all gone astray here except some of the Orders men.'

'You Catholics are a bit funny, you know,' Doctor Henry said. 'Imagine letting them shut chapel doors on your dead, and you just hawking them from door to door beggin' admission. If that was us we'd put in the doors with a sledge, and have a word with the man that shut it.'

'Some awful stories were told in the jail,' The Knife said, 'and there was a rare joke when Doctor Brown was arrested. The Archbishop of Dublin would have silenced a poor curate, but he was afraid of the other men: if only half a dozen like him had come out and got arrested! In Kerry a priest fired on our lads. He will probably get a parish for it.'

'Man alive, if that was Orangemen it happened to!'

'It's the blasted bishops that should be dealt with. Nuala had the right of that, if there had been heed put in her talk they would have been dealt with.'

'Aye, Nuala,' Doctor Henry said, 'Nuala. Man, it is good to think she's outside, free, racing around. I suppose she will miss you, Knife.'

'We were chums,' The Knife said, 'great chums.'

'The like of her comes seldom,' the Doctor said. 'And she would have dealt with the bishops? Aye would she. The quare thing about all this is that all my life I've known, of course, that it is my kind of folk choose your bishops; I mean loyalty to the Empire is as necessary as a mitre to a bishop, and it never seemed a bit of a worry before. It just seemed right that bishops should be our friends, keeping you quiet and threatening hell's blazes if you didn't.

I mind thinking it a fine joke hearing that bishops had agreed to make it a question for Confirmation, "Is it a sin to refuse to pay rent?" And the teachers made certain for their own sake that the children would give the right answer. In here a man sees the cruelty of it.'

'They're a powerful parcel of blackguards all right,' The Knife said; 'and when a priest fights them and gets fired, like Father O'Flanagan, do you know there are some Republicans who think that silenced priests hurt a movement. If all the young priests who have remained right were to pitch the bishops to hell, you'd see something.'

'The priest that was with you and stayed safe is just on the same level with the Free State soldier outside there that is with you but fears to do more than whisper. If a group of them had stood up to the bishops and told the people that they were the half-penny boys of the British Government, then you'd see fun.'

'Well, they didn't; they didn't. Lookin' at it from here it seems all a man can do is spring against it and break.'

'We will have some word from Nuala on Sunday,' the Doctor said. 'Man alive, wouldn't it be great if she could smuggle us in a letter.' And as they let down their beds for the night they talked of the Lagan and of the people that were out there. At the jingle of keys they pretended to be asleep. A crowd of Free State officers came softly in and stood gazing at the faces of the sleepers.

'How little they know; how little they know,' one said, and then again tiptoed out.

The Knife and Doctor Henry were both up on their elbows in the bed.

'You heard that,' The Knife whispered.

'I heard him,' the other said. 'Well, now we know.'

'Now we know,' The Knife agreed, stretching out his hand. It was a mutual, instinctive act. The two men clasped hands for a moment.

'I suppose your death will hurt Nuala a lot?'

'So will yours, Dick; maybe deeper, yours.'

The Doctor drew in a deep breath and was silent. Outside the sentry paced to and fro, and now and then rats scurried behind the partition.

CHAPTER FIFTY-FIVE

NUALA crept up from the bed of the river, and crawled in among the briars at the foot of a rock. Darkness was falling, and a drizzle of rain slavered over the grass. She lay still and waited.

By and by a step sounded from among the trees, and approached leisurely; in soft whistling the *Wearing of the Green* was struck up, and Nuala came out of her hiding-place.

'Let us walk this way,' she said to the Free State officer who had come up to her.

They walked rapidly back towards the river.

'Well?'

'They are to be shot.'

'When?'

'As soon as an incident gives an atmosphere; now everything is ready.'

'And the incident?'

'An officer has been shot; it was one of our own lads shot him, a drunken mix-up, but it has been arranged that at the inquest to-morrow the shooting will be blamed on the Republicans. That's why I sent the message.'

'And will you do nothing?'

'I can do nothing. I'm just dizzy with thinking, but they don't trust me.'

'There must be many soldiers would help The Knife.'

'There's the Orangeman.'

'There will be no rescue then?'

'There will be no rescue; it would be wrong to encourage you to hope.'

'At what time is the execution?'

'At seven; there will be light enough then.'

Her face was turned to the sky, and in the rain it glowed.

'If there was anything I could do, or anything you think I could do,' the officer said fiercely.

She signalled to him to go, and then plunged back across the stream; but he stood there until she was gone, and then after a quick look round, he walked back towards the barracks.

Across on the far side of the river Nuala halted; she sat on a stump of a tree and buried her face in her hands and sobs shook her. She was still sitting there when her father, who had accompanied her on her mission as far as he could, discovered her. He stood silent beside her, a butt of a man, blinking tears out of his eyes.

'It's as we thought,' he said.

She jumped up, and flung her arms around him. 'It's as we thought,' she sobbed.

'God's curse on them,' he prayed.

She clung to his arm and they went across the old track to the boreen where he had the horse and trap.

'Is it . . . in . . . the morning?' he asked.

'No; the next morning.'

'Is it hard on him, do you think?' he asked when they were beside the trap.

'The Knife that was all alive, and Doctor Henry that was so full of interests; it will be hard for them to die.'

'I never put no heed in the talk about men singing going to death; any men'd do that. May hell roast the men that kill The Knife.' Godfrey Dhu rebelled.

They got into the trap, and turned the horse out on the road.

'If there was a horse he could spring on in the morning. Man, if he got his leg across the mare, and a couple of yards start, and the stone walls before him, it would be . . . But where's the use in talking.'

'It's wrong to let The Knife die,' Nuala stormed. 'It's wrong to let him die.'

'The country is drugged,' Godfrey Dhu said; 'the country is drugged.'

The rain grew heavier as they drove and pelted against their faces. They sat very close together, and as they turned up the avenue the old man's arm went across his daughter's shoulder for a moment.

'If I didn't think he would . . . that it was pain to him to die, then being killed wouldn't be so bad.'

There was nobody in the kitchen and the fire was low. Mechanically the old man fixed it up, and drew forward a chair. Nuala sank on the hearth and rested her head against the wall.

'It's not easy to think it is so,' she said.

'I can see it plain enough,' he said; 'I saw it coming. I knew they'd kill him if they caught him.'

The fire crackled, and the blaze danced on the window.

'It's quare to remember him driving the police into the cellar in this very kitchen.'

'And there's nobody to raise a hand now for him. I have a notion if he gets a flash of a chance he'll be out.'

'It would be foolish not to look at the truth without blinkin'; they will herd him close; they hate The Knife, and them that don't are scattered or afraid.'

Sparks flew up the chimney from the blazing fire.

'We should pray,' the old man said. 'We should pray that God will give them both strength so that dying will be easy; for the rest, men that die for Ireland have no need of prayer.'

'Let us pray then,' she said, getting to her knees.

When the rosary was ended, Nuala lay crumpled against the wall. The old man, after some minutes of silent prayer, rose slowly to sit on a creepy in the corner. Neither spoke. Rain pelted on the window, the dog crawled over to snuggle at the old man's feet, and then, with a jerk, his head went up and he growled. There were steps in the street, outside the door, and the dog dived across the floor growling. Godfrey Dhu got wearily to his feet, and when he opened the door he stood still, waiting for the visitor to show up. Then he took a pace out into the night. The dog rubbed against his leg and gurned.

Nuala came quickly to the door, and went out on the street. Something whizzed past her head, and thudded against the wall, a piece of earth, a sod of turf, or some such thing.

'Come on inside,' Nuala said, taking her father's arm. She bolted the door behind them; children were encouraged to attack them thus.

'Would they let us see him?' he asked, after a long reverie.

'They would not let us see him,' she said. 'And it would only be worse anyway.'

'If the old men could do anything . . .'

'There's nothing old men could do.'

'Is it a hard thing for him to die? I try to see what it must be for him to die; to walk out to be killed at The Knife's age. Do you think it will be hard for him?'

'No man will know that,' she said. 'And Doctor Henry too.'

'It's a wonder the Orangemen let Doctor Henry die.'

Nuala's body stiffened, and rose slowly from its tired droop; her father's gaze was still on the fire.

'It's a wonder the Orangemen let Doctor Henry die,' she murmured to herself. 'Maybe it was God put that thought in your mind,' she said, moving quickly to him on her knees. 'Maybe it was God.' Her face was very close to his, and her eyes flashed with excitement. She jumped to her feet, and the old man rose too.

'What are you going to do?' he asked in a whisper.

'I'm going to Sam Rowan.' She was drawing on a dry coat.

'I'll go with you,' he said. After a pause she nodded, and held out his coat for him, and gave him his stick. They went out into the rain together.

CHAPTER FIFTY-SIX

NUALA and her father had made their way across the fields to the laneway that went round to the back of Rowans. The rain had ceased as they walked, black clouds raced to the west. Neither spoke.

She pushed open the gate and waited for the dog to bark; she wondered he had not barked already when her father came heavy-footed up the lane that skirted the yard. There was no light shining in the back windows; the family was as yet in the kitchen in the front, she thought, as she waited for her father to come across the gap between them.

'I thought it was you,' a voice called softly out of the darkness, and Sam Rowan came forward, with his hand on Carabine's collar.

'It's us,' Nuala said.

Sam shook hands with Godfrey Dhu.

'There's nobody in the kitchen,' he explained, and led the way in. He stood with his back to the fire and waited.

'They're going to kill The Knife and Doctor Henry the other morrow morning.'

Sam nodded.

'You knew?'

'I knew.'

Godfrey Dhu stirred slightly on his feet.

Nuala walked up until only a pace separated them.

'You could lead the Orangemen of the Lagan into a rescue,' she said.

'They think a lot of Doctor Henry,' he agreed.

'You could lead them into a rescue,' she repeated.

'There's some of them would put heed in what I'd say.'

'You could lead them into a rescue.'

'They would be willin' to free the Doctor.'

'And does The Knife being with him, stop them?'

'They would be a lot quicker if he was by himself.'

'Will it stop them?'

'Are you asking me to rescue The Knife and Doctor Henry?'

'As I never wanted to ask a thing in my life, Sam. But only if you can see that it can be done.'

'Orangemen could do a lot if they had their minds strong on it.'

'Then, Sam, you'll set their minds strong on it?'

'It won't be my fault if The Knife and Doctor Henry is shot,' he said simply.

Tears flicked out of Nuala's eyes on her blinking lashes.

'Can you get any word for us when and how it is to be done?'

'They will be shot in the gravel pit up near the edge of the wood at seven o'clock.'

'Could we be sure of that? So as to build on it.'

'Big Micheal told me, and he will tell me if there is a change.'

'I'll go round among the neighbours, and will you be at home all day?' Sam said.

'I'll be at home,' she said.

Sam picked up his coat off a peg on the wall. Godfrey Dhu went out without a word.

'I'll be waiting for you, Sam,' Nuala said.

'I'll come to you,' Sam Rowan said.

Nuala turned quickly and walked out.

CHAPTER FIFTY-SEVEN

Phil Burns came in out of the fields. He had been making a drain, and his clothes were plastered with mud.

He came slowly across the green, his coat over his arm. Rain would fall soon, he noticed, glancing up at the sky, and round at the butt of the wind. There were cattle bunched inside the gate at Godfrey Dhu's; an old man and a girl there that were full of worries and uneasiness. Denis Freel was roofing a hen house; he would go across to Denis when he'd had a cup of tea and dry socks.

He was in the street before he noticed the motor-car at the gable, and just then he heard voices inside. He frowned; had he noticed the car he would have delayed his coming in. Excited voices, he noted, as he drew near, and he quickened his steps.

James was inside, and a local doctor; a likeable sort that doctor, and Phil was relieved. There were three or four others in the party.

'Captain Curran was killed. What is their rascality going to stop at?' Molly exclaimed.

Phil Burns stood in the middle of the floor and took off his hat. 'God rest poor Eddie Curran's soul. Too bad, too bad.'

'It was just murder; just murder,' Molly said.

'Shot on out of the dark like wild geese. No wonder the whole country is stirred up over it.'

'It means that we have been too soft with them,' James said. 'They think they can do anything, and that we'll stay our hand; well, they're wrong this time.'

'It would be the price of them if an example was made,' Molly encouraged. 'Poor Captain Curran; everybody thought he would go with the Godfrey Dhus, but faith no.'

'Sureties wouldn't back his bill again if he did,' Phil said.

'An' are you in the soldiers now?' he continued, turning to the Doctor.

'I was at the inquest.'

'Sure the Doctor is the coroner,' Molly said.

'An' what did you say about Curran?' Phil asked.

'A verdict of wilful murder against the three Reds that's still left about the mountain.'

'An' when was the killin' done?'

'Last night; about midnight.'

'Then the three Reds didn't do it?'

'Aye, but they did,' James said.

The Doctor moved uneasily on his feet; James Burns put a hand on his shoulder.

'The Reds murdered Curran, and The Knife and Doctor Henry will pay for it; to-morrow morning the papers will have it, and next morning the world will see the reply.'

'I told you them three men had no hand or part in the shooting.'

'What in the name of God would you know about it?' Molly demanded. 'Hold your tongue, and don't be making a show of us all,' she pleaded.

'They had no hand in it,' the old man maintained, 'and I can swear it. You, you big bag of farts,' he stormed, turning towards the coroner, 'are you to rise the stink so that the best man in the Lagan can be smothered?'

'I won't have any more of that sort of talk,' James blustered.

The old man raised his hand above his head. 'I swear before God that the men you say had no part in that killin', for I know . . .'

'I told you . . .' the Doctor began.

'Shut up,' Burns ordered. 'Come on, let us get out of here.'

Phil Burns blocked his son's passage to the door. 'You are not going to murder The Knife,' he said very quietly.

'He should have been shot long ago.'

Phil Burns grabbed his son by the throat. 'If you don't swear to God . . .'

'Let go,' James stormed.

'Swear.'

'Let go.'

'Swear.'

James tried to drag himself clear. The father made a drive to force him into the room; Molly flung herself on them both.

'Damn you, father,' James cried, and struck the old man in the face.

'James, James,' Molly said. 'For God's sake, James, can't you promise.'

'I will not promise.' He made a violent effort to break free. He crashed against the room door, and he butted the old man with his head; his hold never slackened, and his braced body pressed James back towards the door. Again James struck and, breaking the old man's hold, he dived for the door, his father crashing on the floor.

'Jesus Christ, Brig., if he goes round telling that . . . You must stop the execution,' the coroner fussed.

'Ah, hump you,' James exploded, glad to vent his anger; he struck the coroner with his fist in the mouth, and then sprang into his car and drove off.

CHAPTER FIFTY-EIGHT

A SOLDIER flung the morning paper into the cell; little acts like this had sprung up all round the jail routine. The Doctor, lying on his bed, turned the pages. Presently he whistled softly. The Knife looked up; he was making a mat.

'The stage is set. They had an inquest yesterday on poor Eddie Curran; there's a fine speech here from the coroner, and it would cover half a dozen executions.'

'You think that was just preparing the people's mind?'

'Don't leave any doubt in your mind, Knife; you're for it.'

'They'll never dare shoot you, Dick.'

'Aye will they. Play-acting at being the National Army, aren't they? It will be as good as a coat of green paint to them to get a solid Orangeman like me to shoot.'

'Well, we're not dead yet,' The Knife said.

'Knife, I tell you, you will go before the firing party to-morrow; now just take in that idea without any blinking.'

The Knife got to his feet. 'What do you want me to do, Dick; bawl out? I'm not kiddin' myself.'

The Doctor tapped his pipe against his heel, and

neither spoke for some time. 'Strange how things thin out; there's nothing happening, we are just waiting, and everything is at rest.'

'I know what's coming. I tell myself, and then when I tell it to myself and listen I get a feelin' I don't understand what I'm saying to myself. Here they come.' The Knife sat down on his bed.

There was a tramp of feet in the corridor, the cell door was opened, and a crowd of officers came in.

'Prisoners, 'shun!' the sergeant of the guard called.

The prisoners gave no heed.

'Your execution has been ordered to take place to-morrow morning at seven o'clock,' the Governor said, when the officers had ringed round the prisoners.

'I have to complain again that the cell is too close to the latrines,' the Doctor said quietly. 'Prisoners should not be kept here, their health might be permanently injured.'

'Aye, and I have complained that the windows are not kept clear; just look at that, an inch deep of dirt; it makes the cell dark.'

'Overcrowding is to be discouraged under the circumstances,' the Doctor continued. 'Perhaps you chaps would go to blazes and leave us to ourselves.'

'We will see whether you have so much old lip out of you in the morning,' Burns growled.

'Been scrapin' your face against barbed wire, James,' the Doctor mocked.

'I'll not take chat from you,' Burns stormed.

'Burns,' The Knife said quietly.

'Well, Knife?' Burns said.

'I just want to say, James, that you are about the

meanest scut that ever breathed; a lying, perjured rat. And if you don't get out of this cell now . . .'

'I suppose you'll see a priest now, when you're up against it,' James sneered, and went out.

The other officers followed.

'Morbid lot. Anxious to see how we'd take it; I had a pain in my breakfast for a minute,' the Doctor said.

'Well, it's there now, plain and straight and hard.'

'If a man panicked in a hole like this, afraid of what was coming, it would be a terrible thing,' the Doctor mused. 'I've seen patients panic from a death sentence; trapped like this, panic would be hell.'

'There's nothing to panic over,' The Knife said sharply.

'To be sure there's nothing to panic over, nothing.'

'It's a mercy they didn't rope Rowan into it too.'

'Rowan wouldn't be afraid, Knife.'

'Nuala and Rowan will know about it.'

'I must write a letter for Sam, there's a few things I have to settle.'

'I'll write a note or two myself,' The Knife said.

They sat apart, facing opposite ways.

'Is there anything I can do, Knife?' the sergeant of the guard asked, putting his head in the door.

'Can you get us out of this?'

'I can't do that.'

'Then you can do nothing.'

Silence.

'Knife.'

'Well, sentry.'

'Can I take out a message?'

'No.'

'Can I do anything for you?'

'Can you get us out?'

'No.'

'Then you can do nothing.'

Silence.

The little sheath over the spy-hole in the cell door stirred, somebody was peeping in to see how men who are going to die pass the time. The Knife got up and pasted a piece of paper on the glass.

The Knife delayed his letters; he turned his thoughts on preparation for death; he had always prepared more or less for death, a habit; mostly every night of his life he had said prayers for a happy death. Now, urgent, all-compelling thoughts of death stirred in him. He prayed silently, vaguely uneasy. How easy it would be to die if he were to be permitted confession; how easy to die then. He began an exhaustive examination of conscience.

'The priest is here to see you, Knife,' the warder said, opening the cell door. The corridor outside was thronged with soldiers to escort the condemned man across the yard.

'I'll be brought back here ?' he inquired.

The officer nodded, and The Knife followed him out.

The priest was in a large room; there was a bright fire and two chairs in it.

The chaplain was Father Burns.

'Won't you sit down so that we may talk first.'

The Knife sat down.

'I'm sorry to see you come to this, Knife.'

'Sounds a bit queer; we can't both win, and you're not on my side.'

'I am on your side now,' the priest said quietly. 'I am with the penitent preparing to meet his God.'

'Will we have mass in the morning?'

The priest nodded.

'I'd be glad to serve mass,' The Knife said. 'It's a long time now since I served mass.'

Again the priest nodded. 'You see how deep religion is really, and how foolish it is ever to lose sight of the last end. I knew you would come back to your faith in your last moments.'

The Knife smiled, was about to speak, but waited.

'You should use your influence now that death brings you close to God to warn others outside who are yet blinded to give up their evil ways.'

'Now just what do you mean?'

'There are men outside still resisting the teaching of our holy bishops.'

'Holy bishops? I am going to be shot to-morrow, and before God to-day I think the bishops are guilty of that murder.'

The priest blessed himself. 'Unfortunate man, with death staring you in the face, do you still resist God's mercy?'

'I do not want to fight with you; hear my confession and let me go.'

'But can't you see? I can't hear your confession unless you accept the teaching of our holy bishops.'

'On what?'

'On this unhappy quarrel.'

'The bishops are the agents of the British Empire.'

'I can't listen to such talk.' The priest and The Knife both got to their feet.

'Is there any Catholic priest left in the Lagan,

Father, or have you all deserted us? Would not some of the Order priests be allowed in?'

'There are a few blackguards among the clergy; you must be saved from them. What hope of repentance could be held out if a priest of God encouraged you in your sin? You will get no other chaplain but me.'

'Then I'll grope my own way to heaven.'

'Tell me, do you even die in charity with all men?'

'I'm not feelin' over charitable to them that's murderin' me.'

'It is no murder.'

The Knife shrugged his shoulders and was silent.

'Do you die with hatred in your heart; do you have bad feeling against those whose duty it is to kill you?'

'I have hard feelings against them; why shouldn't I?'

'James feels keenly having to do this.'

'James is windy.'

'Will you pray there for some minutes? I'll go out to the chapel and pray for you; you have yet time, but it's fleeting.'

'I have to pray for myself, Father, and have little time to pray for you now. Will you at least say mass in the morning?'

'I'll celebrate mass at six,' the priest said.

The Knife walked out, and was taken back to his cell.

CHAPTER FIFTY-NINE

It was evening when Sam Rowan came across the river to meet Nuala Godfrey Dhu. She was waiting for him, pacing restlessly among the trees. He came slowly down the open fields, striding with a carelessness that she knew was feigned, and from which she drew hope. His head came up with a jerk when he became aware of her presence, and he breathed in sharply. He strode quickly towards her, his fists clenched. Her eyes flashed, her lips parted, and her face suddenly flooded with colour. He was silent until he came to a halt and his fingers closed around the hands she instinctively held out to him.

'We'll do it,' he said.

'Sam Rowan,' she breathed, 'Sam Rowan.'

From behind them in the trees came the stamp of old Godfrey Dhu; he too had been waiting. They gave no heed to his approach until he came up beside them.

'We'll do it,' Sam Rowan repeated.

The old man cleared his throat a few times, and then without a word his hand touched the interlocked fingers of his companions. All three walked back to the house in silence.

'The two inside will know nothing,' Godfrey Dhu said.

'It is better so,' Sam decided.

The old man stamped across to his corner, and Sam Rowan sat on a chair. The fire blazed sturdily under the kettle, Nuala knelt on the hearth. Nobody spoke. Sam noticed how a pulse throbbed in Nuala's throat: Doctor Henry deserved her, he thought.

'Let me make tea for you, Sam,' Nuala said.

'I'm wantin' tea right enough.'

'It'll be a long night,' Godfrey Dhu said.

'It'll be short for them,' Nuala said quickly.

'I suppose it's as well they don't know,' Godfrey Dhu said.

'It's better they don't know,' Sam Rowan said. And again they were silent.

The kettle spurted water, and Nuala wet the tea.

'I'll just have a drink,' Nuala said, 'I'll eat nothing.'

'I'm going to have a good feed,' Sam said, 'and you'll not come unless you eat too, Nuala.'

'Then I'll eat,' she said, smiling.

'It's quare how little a body has to say,' Sam commented.

'I can only see the two of them waiting inside,' Nuala said. 'And then I see you gathering, and then I nearly choke when I begin to see the two pictures coming close.'

'It will be midnight before we start,' Sam said.

'And I can come, Sam?' Nuala pleaded.

'I thought I'd go early to make sure the wood was empty; and I knew you'd rather be there . . .'

'Rather be there?' Nuala murmured.

'I could meet you at the foot bridge at eleven,' Sam said.

The clock ticked steadily and the fire blazed. All three were standing.

The old man came across the hearth. 'Ye think ye'll be able to do it?' he asked huskily.

'Am as sure as I'm standing here,' Sam said.

Godfrey Dhu turned to face his daughter, and his face broke into a smile.

'Am sorry they don't know it inside,' he said, raising his voice. Nuala thrilled to the new ring in it.

'Hush,' she said, putting her finger on her lips.

'At eleven then,' Sam Rowan whispered. He went quickly out.

CHAPTER SIXTY

SAM was waiting. He came out from among the grey rocks, and Nuala halted until he called. She put her arm through his, and without speaking they entered the wood. When the path narrowed, Sam took her hand and led the way to the resting-place he had selected. When the lights of the barracks sparkled through the trees, Nuala's grasp tightened on Sam's fingers. He moved very cautiously in among high boulders.

'They're behind some of those lights,' Nuala said.

'I'm wondering if there's a sentry along here,' Sam whispered.

'Halt! Who goes there?'

The challenge came very sharply out of the dark, and Sam craned his neck for the exchange of words that followed. A second challenge farther away rang out a few minutes later. A long silence. The next challenge was faint from distance.

Standing under the shelter of the rock he could see her face at his shoulder. She was leaning forward, listening, her body inclined away from his. She breathed deeply, and her body relaxed against the rock. She stumbled slightly and bumped against him. He put his arm around her shoulders, and she leaned against him. She moved her head, her hair tickled his nose, and the whiff of it drew his face down closer. He stiffened and his arm dropped from her shoulders.

'It won't be long till they come,' he whispered. 'If Doctor Henry knew you were out here,' Sam added after a pause.

'I was remembering who it is means to do the killin',' Nuala whispered.

'Let us sit down,' Rowan suggested. He sat down and made a place for her beside him. 'He had been only showin' off before you.'

'Men have some manliness of their own.'

'Doctor Henry wouldn't be in there only for you,' Sam added.

'Don't say next that you wouldn't be out here, only for me,' she pleaded.

'And why else?' Sam asked.

Nuala groaned, and would have risen, but his arm pinned her. 'But Doctor Henry is your cousin,' she said.

'Doctor Henry's a man I think a lot of, and I've cousins I don't think much of: but I wouldn't have thought of it if you hadn't asked me, and the way the others put agin it I'd have dropped it only you had to be faced.'

'I can't bear having it all put down on me; and I couldn't think of you that's so strong and cold doin' anythin' that wasn't from inside yourself.'

He got quickly to his feet, and she tumbled out on the grass. He made no attempt to help her up.

'If it had a been me inside and Doctor Henry outside . . .' Sam said.

'Then nobody could have roused the Lagan,' she

said simply. 'It took you. Doctor Henry would have tried, but the men wouldn't follow him.'

'You know a lot about Orangemen,' Sam said gruffly.

'It took a deep, strong call to pull them,' she said. 'Only you could have done it, Sam Rowan. Hush,' she said quickly, grabbing his arm.

'They're comin'; stay you here.' He went off quickly, and she was left alone.

Her talk with Sam had torn her; in her tiredness she could not support the responsibilities he would pour on her. Burns her plaything; she shuddered now when she thought of him, his white face and fair hair, his kisses. He had not been her plaything; he had been playing for something; if it was a situation, and he had got it. Sam blamed her for Doctor Henry; blame was not the word, Sam didn't blame her for anything, just said the thing was so, and that was all. She was pausing to examine herself in relation to Doctor Henry when the thought leapt into light in her mind; Rowan had said he was there only because of her. She clenched her fists and stood very erect now among the boulders. It took a deep call to gather the Orangemen; only Sam Rowan could have made it; was it she had called to Sam? Her body tingled with excitement, and she leaned towards the whispers in among the trees.

'Sam,' she said softly to herself, 'Sam.'

He came towards her again. 'They're all crowding in; they'll crawl up close and hide at their ease. Most like The Knife and Dick will be blindfold; you'll go down when I say it, and tear off the cloth and lead them back quick into the trees.'

'I'll do that,' she said simply.

'We're no wantin' it to be thought Orangemen did this; we want to be left alone,' Sam said.

'You're a man of peace, Sam,' she said. She was suddenly light-hearted, and she saw Sam's teeth as he smiled.

'It's easy as kiss your hand,' Sam said.

'But it's wonderful, Sam.'

'I suppose you'll marry Doctor Henry,' Sam said after a pause.

'Me! Marry Doctor Henry?' She chilled out the rising excitement. 'What under God makes you say that, Sam Rowan?'

'Don't you like Doctor Henry?' Sam asked.

'Not in that way, Sam,' she whispered.

'Then who, in the name of Christ, do you like?' he muttered, swinging her round to face him. Their eyes met across the short patch of gloom, and then, a-tremble, she was in his arms.

'I'll blot them off the face of the earth,' Sam said, when he released her, and he bounded away to arrange another group of Orangemen who had arrived for the rescue.

CHAPTER SIXTY-ONE

NIGHT-TIME in the jail; lights washed out through the barred windows into the moonlight; lights streamed out into the night from the windows of the barracks. Sentries paced to and fro, stepping sharply.

The condemned men let down their beds; they did not undress beyond taking off their boots and coats. They spoke little. Now and then when their eyes met they smiled, sometimes wan smiles, sometimes smiles of genuine amusement.

'Did you ever think a man could have so many thoughts in one night?' The Knife said once.

The Doctor nodded gently.

'A man could get himself settled down to sleep, if he liked,' The Knife said later.

'It would be a waste of life,' Doctor Henry said.

The Knife nodded, he was fingering the cross on his rosary beads. He got down on his knees, and burying his face in his hands he prayed. When he got off his knees the Doctor was quietly smoking.

'I wonder are we doing anything more than just dying,' Doctor Henry mused. 'Are we building anything?'

'One of the warders says there will be bonfires.'

'I don't believe a word of it,' Doctor Henry said.

Outside a sentry challenged a passer-by. The Doctor wound his watch.

'I'll label this for the Reverend Mr. Gregg; a

decent old sort; I had to console him last evening. I told him I wouldn't want him in the morning.'

'Father Burns will say mass at six. He says that an Orders priest wouldn't be let in because he would only harden me in my sin.'

'Mulcahy said the same thing in parliament,' the Doctor said, amused. 'What mean little minds these chaps have. When a small mind invokes a bad temper and holds it in front to bark at his enemies he is liable to do stupid things.'

The Knife made no reply.

'That was a hell of a mouthful,' the Doctor said with a grin. 'I tell you if I spent a couple of days dying I'd be a marvel to the world.'

'We're getting too far away from the job in front,' the Knife said. 'I want to keep my mind fixed and at peace.'

'It's no time for being smart,' the Doctor said. 'Though mind you I think it's wise I was.' He glanced round at The Knife and smiled; The Knife was not looking his way, however, and the Doctor, sighing gently, rested his chin on his hand.

'Would you care for a cup of tea?' the orderly officer asked.

'Yes, let us have it. And, hello, get a table and real cups and some home-made bread, will you?' Now what put an idea like that in my head, the Doctor mused, when the officer withdrew.

'You should have told him to put the butter in a dish, a big meascan, to give us the bannock of bread uncut,' The Knife said. 'But I can't take any tea,' he said hastily.

'I really don't want it either,' the Doctor said, getting to his feet. 'Hello, sentry!'

The sentry came to the door.

'Please tell the orderly officer that we won't have any tea; it's an unhealthy practice. Thank him.'

The sentry saluted; the Doctor withdrew from the door.

'What time is it?' The Knife asked.

'It's ten minutes to four.'

The Knife glanced at the window. 'It will soon be daylight.'

'It will soon be daylight,' the Doctor agreed.

'It's easy, Dick.'

'It's easy, Knife.'

'Ever hear of Robert Emmet, Knife?' the Doctor asked after a long pause.

'A little,' The Knife said, smiling.

'It must have been hard to be waiting,' the Doctor said, a little huskily.

'It would be hard to be waiting,' The Knife said softly; he too was on his feet.

'It's four o'clock, Knife.'

'It's four o'clock, Dick.'

'It will be daylight in an hour.'

'In an hour.'

'So there is no use waiting any more, Knife.'

'No use, Dick,' The Knife whispered.

They shook hands solemnly; The Knife put his back to the door, Doctor Henry put his back to the wall opposite.

'It's easy.'

'To be sure it's easy.'

'What a game men play; every time the sentry challenged I held my breath.'

'Me too.'

'Nuala: I'm sure she did her best,' The Knife said.

'Aye, and Sam. Sam would be prancing to do anything he could for her. When Sam warms up . . . But will he? Maybe he will go back again into the dull brown world of the Lagan and shut his eyes.'

'I thought a lot of Sam that night we went into him about Hugh.'

'So that's how you think of that night. The Lagan holds that night to your credit.'

'Well, good luck to the Lagan; they'll have to puzzle it out.'

'Good luck to the Lagan, Knife.'

'Do you think she knew?'

'She was sure to know.'

'Day is streaking in.'

'It was a short night.'

'It just melted like anything.'

'Still, it's easy.'

'To be sure it's easy.'

'Mass will be on soon,' the orderly officer called in.

'Will you come back straight here, Knife?'

'I'll come straight back,' The Knife said, getting ready to shave.

The priest was vestmented and waiting when The Knife reached the little chapel. A number of Free State officers were already kneeling. The prisoner went straight up to the altar rail, and took his stand beside the priest.

'In nomine patris et filii et spiritus sanctus . . .'

With quiet, steady voice The Knife spoke the responses. His mind opened to allow the full story of the sacrifice to unfold; strength gained in him as he prayed and he was eager for the Elevation, waiting;

a sense of nearness and peace such as he had never known. Mechanically he tinkled the bell.

When there was a movement behind him he woke up from his deep contemplation. Free State officers were moving towards the altar rails. He glanced back and his eye noticed the men as they approached. The first was the provost marshal. Mechanically he began *Confiteor deo.*

The priest turned to face his congregation, the sacred host in his fingers.

'Domine non sum dignus . . .'

The Knife struck his breast. As the priest came down the altar he raised his head, hoping . . . the priest passed on. In one mighty rush the prayerfulness that had held him during the Elevation swept back into his soul, and he did not notice that the priest had returned to the altar and was waiting, awkward.

'Come at least spiritually . . .'

Very quietly an officer tiptoed up, and served the priest at the last ablution; mass was finished. The officers sat back on their seats to see him pass out. The priest came quickly out of the sacristy without his vestments. The Knife still knelt before the altar. Very slowly he got to his feet, genuflected, and then with a steady stride he walked down the aisle. At the door the priest interrupted him.

'Have you nothing further to say to me?' he asked quietly.

'Nothing,' The Knife said.

The priest stood aside, and let him pass back to his cell.

CHAPTER SIXTY-TWO

Two soldiers entered the cell with a small table, covered with a white tablecloth. Two chairs were taken in, and then followed a tray with a breakfast.

'They have brought the home-made bread,' the Doctor said.

'And the print of butter,' The Knife noticed.

'If there is anything else now,' the orderly officer asked, pausing on his way to the door.

'We are all right, thank you.'

The Doctor poured out the tea.

'It seems strange to eat, meaningless, doesn't it?'

'I'm thirsty,' the Doctor said. 'And we'll eat just to show them.'

'What does it matter what they think?' The Knife asked.

'It does. There's our folk. We're before the footlights.'

'I'm anxious to keep my mind at rest as it is.'

'It will be soon now.'

'It will be soon. I'm glad it's out in the sun, out in the air,' The Knife said. 'It's a healthier place to die in,' he added with a smile.

'You're making a fine breakfast, Knife. It's a pity we haven't an audience.'

The Doctor filled out another cup of tea to each

of them. 'Here's to the two of us, Knife. We're just as sturdy a pair of heroes as you could find.'

'If dying twice would get you free, Dick,' The Knife said tensely.

'Sure, Knife, I know it makes it harder for you. Thinking you dragged me in; but you didn't, and if you had itself I'd be glad to be in now. I'd never have known what a remarkably fine fellow I was if I hadn't a chance to be a hero. I should make a speech now. Doctor Henry's farewell to the Lagan.'

'All right, Dick, I just wanted you to know.'

'Fine, Knife. Now let me talk. I dragged you into my own house, thinking you would be safe, of course, but in at the root I was being a fine fellow before Nuala; if I hadn't brought you in . . .'

'I'd have choked out in that black hole of Cormac's,' The Knife said.

'All right, the big fact we can't change is that we're here.'

There was a tramp of feet in the corridor.

'Deep down and through and through I'm at peace,' Doctor Henry said.

'I'm as clear-minded as the rising sun,' The Knife said, linking his arm in the Doctor's.

The cell door opened. The provost marshal came in; behind him were other officers.

'The unpleasant duty of the morning falls on me,' he said. 'I would like to ask your forgiveness for what I have to do.'

There was a silence in the cell.

'Knife, you would not die holding a mean grudge?'

'It's not to me you must answer.'

'Make your peace within yourself,' the Doctor

said. 'I'm not giving any anæsthetic in this operation.'

'It's not my fault,' the provost marshal began.

'Argue that out with your masters.'

'My masters are the Irish people.'

'Some day they will kill you for this,' The Knife said quietly.

There was again a long silence in the cell; someone among the officers sighed deeply.

The Knife and Doctor Henry faced each other again and smiled, their handcuffed hands locked; they were of a height and the morning sun spilling in through a corner of the window warmed their glowing faces; neither spoke.

The procession moved off. Two prisoners, side by side, stepping slowly, came out into the open air, the sun over the hilltops shone warm against their faces. The crowing of cocks came from the village, and near by a river gurgled. For a moment the prisoners paused, and then following the inexorable pull on their arms, moved forward, gravel under foot, gravel. The Knife's lips moved, and he murmured to himself. The pull slackened, and instinctively the two stood erect, shoulders touching . . .

And then crash . . .

CHAPTER SIXTY-THREE

A VOLLEY from the trees jerked the firing party out of its rigid stand, and they collapsed in a jumble. Before the spectators could thaw out of their horror bullets ripped among them. Somebody dived across for shelter and those who were able to free themselves from the spell dashed after him.

The prisoners stood very rigid; they were now deadly pale, and swayed slightly as they stood.

'Knife, Doctor Henry.' Nuala's voice swept across the void, and life leapt with a bound, flooding the mind with excitement that set the bodies a-tremble. Her fingers tore at the bandages and they blinked at the light; the sun had been shining on them. She took their hands and they ran with her into the trees.

'You gave us a lot of bother,' Sam Rowan greeted, taking a hand of each.

'I was thinking you'd be that busy with the spring work you'd have to put it back for a wet morning,' Doctor Henry said.

'Maybe if we tried a wee trot across the fields,' The Knife said.

'You'll meet some folk up near Cormac's,' Sam said.

He stood with Nuala's hand in his as he spoke. The Knife paid no heed. Doctor Henry took a quick step towards them, and locked his hands around theirs, and raced off after The Knife.

Up on the side of the mountain Doctor Henry and The Knife lay down on the crinkly heather and rested. Below the Lagan shimmered in a haze of heat, and whitewashed walls flashed in the sunlight. In the distance a train whistled. Suddenly a dark cloud of smoke leapt up amid the glow and a roar boomed through the Lagan.

'Bang goes Godfrey Dhu's,' The Knife said.

'And bang goes Doctor Henry's,' the Doctor cheered, anticipating the boom that followed a second puff. 'It's poor satisfaction to them.'

A lorry passed on the road below.

'Let us get back up into the mountains,' The Knife said. 'We'll be safe there.'

'Sam deserves her,' the Doctor said, his gaze on the Lagan. 'Good luck to the two of you,' he waved. The ball of smoke had now banked out, and was tearing into ribbons along the fringe, and excited voices were calling loudly through the Lagan.

'Doctor Henry crosses the mountains. It was only a stream that chap Cæsar crossed,' the Doctor said.

'It was dead easy, Dick.'

'Like kiss your hand, Knife.'

And with a whoop they went racing across the heather towards the mountains that here and there flashed back the sun.